Looking for
the Possible Dance

Also by A. L. Kennedy

Night Geometry and the Garscadden Trains

A. L. Kennedy

Looking for
the Possible Dance

Minerva

A Minerva Paperback
LOOKING FOR THE POSSIBLE DANCE

First published in Great Britain 1993
by Martin Secker & Warburg Ltd
This Minerva edition published 1994
by Mandarin Paperbacks
an imprint of Reed Consumer Books Ltd
Michelin House, 81 Fulham Road, London SW3 6RB
and Auckland, Melbourne, Singapore and Toronto

Reprinted 1994 (twice)

Copyright © A. L. Kennedy 1993
The author has asserted his moral rights

A CIP catalogue record for this title
is available from the British Library
ISBN 0 7493 9758 6

Printed and bound in Great Britain
by Cox & Wyman Ltd, Reading, Berks

For M. Price, J. H. Price, E. M. Kennedy
and my friends who rarely fail,
with my love

'Everything else is a waste of time. Do you hear me? Everything else is a waste of time. You hear me, Margaret? You understand?'

Margaret was outside in the night, standing behind the Methodist Church Hall. Her ears, numbed after hours of music, were rushing with the sudden quiet, as if she had just dipped her head inside a sea-shell, or a big tin box. Margaret's father was sitting on two empty beer crates, breathing in and out enormously, his legs extended flat ahead of him and both his hands folded, hotly, round one of her wrists.

'See, there's the moon, Princess. Do you see?'

'Yes.'

His swaying finger seemed to nudge at the fat, white circle; leave a little mark.

'And there is The Plough – one, two, three, four and a little tail, and there's . . . there's . . . Orion is up there, too. Stars and stars and stars, more stars behind these stars and, if you could see all the stars, the sky would be white. All of that, up there. Mi-rac-u-lous. And they see us, Margaret. Princess. They see us. The moon looks down at us and we look up at her and it's wonderful. She's telling us, "Everything else is a waste of time." That's what she says. You hear her? That's what she says.'

Margaret watched her daddy, smiling with his eyes closed against the moonlight as he squeezed her hand. She stepped up and kissed his ear and was a little worried about him in case he took cold from sitting out with no coat on. She also wondered what he meant.

Beginning with her wondering, or the cold, or the beautiful plume of her father's breath which clouded up to make small rainbows around the moon, Margaret often remembers that night. It was the only time that she and her father went out together like that. Formally. Why he wanted to dance with Methodists, in that hall, on that night, she does not know, but it was wonderful, all the same.

Resting her weight down carefully on to his feet, her daddy walked and span her through the two-step and into the waltz, round and round. She closed her eyes and rested in against his stomach, the bright shirt, the smell of his soap and himself and a new aftershave.

Even better was to sit with a glass of orange juice in a place where she could watch her father dance away without her. He drew her eye; surely, everyone's eye. And they all knew where to look for the blue of his suit. The suit she had never seen before and would not see again until after her father was dead.

The sets formed up and separated in and out of rings and lines, her father somehow always at their heart. Margaret had never seen him so graceful, stepping and sliding as if it were all that he ever did or could ever want to do. Among the swirl of unimportant heads, she would see her father's face, perhaps smiling at her, his eyes glowing blue with the dance. Or maybe she would glimpse the back of his head with its fine, grey hair which reminded her of the soft fur on a cat.

Whenever a ceilidh is mentioned now, or any kind of dance,

somewhere in her mind, Margaret will compare it with the never repeated Anniversary Ceilidh at the Methodist Church Hall and the blue light it called to her father's eyes.

She only once asked why they didn't go dancing again. She was out with her father, one afternoon, cleaning up the allotment for the summer to come in.

'Och, I never liked dancing, honey. It makes my feet hurt.'

That was a lie. He could never have danced the way that he did with sore feet. And he'd enjoyed himself, she could tell.

'You'll be old enough soon to go on your own. You'll like that.'

'I wanted to go with you.'

'Would you want me to have sore feet.'

'Were your feet really sore?'

'I was really sore. I wouldn't like to be that sore again.'

A blackbird chuck-chucked away over the fence for a reason they couldn't see.

'What did you mean about it being a waste of time?'

'Sorry, love?'

'What did you mean about it being a waste of time? You said when we were looking at the moon that everything else was a waste of time.'

'I don't remember that.'

She waited to see if he would notice he had lied again. He coughed and then looked at her.

'The moon makes me say silly things. It does that to folk. Sometimes.'

'What did you mean, but?'

'Och, I don't know. I can't even think what I said.'

Such lies.

Margaret's father stared at the lavender bushes and grubbed his hoe along the clean, black soil between them. There weren't

3

any weeds. The earth was never left long enough to grow them. He smiled down at the strange, ashy plants.

'Your mother planted those when you were three.'

Margaret brushed her hand through the flowers, breathing in their grey and purple smell; not knowing why her father told such lies. Things that weren't all that important, but still were not true. The lavender bushes, for example, had come in the springtime, last year. Margaret remembered her father had brought home the seedlings and planted them. Carefully, in the evening, with water before and after, so they wouldn't die. Margaret's mother hadn't been there. Margaret hadn't even seen her mother in years: couldn't remember her ever being anywhere at all, although she must have had a mother, naturally. Everyone did.

Her daddy blinked into the sun.

'You can make lavender bags in the autumn; you can sew them. You can sew? Margaret?'

At school, if anyone told her lies, Margaret wouldn't speak to them, but Daddy was different. He was always more convinced by his stories than anyone else. And because she wanted to please her father, to oblige, Margaret tried to believe him as much as she could. This seemed to make him happy, which meant she could be happy too.

Margaret smelled the lavender smell along her fingers.

'I suppose I could practise sewing. We don't really do that much. We knit. You can't knit lavender bags?'

'Naah. All the lavender would fall out.'

'So I could just knit empty bags, then, and save time.'

He stroked his hand down over her head and she looked up at the shine of his big, white face. He was smiling a little bit and his nose was starting to redden from the sun.

'You know when we looked at the moon.'

4

'Yes, I know.'

'I said that everything *else* was a waste of time.'

'Yes, I know that.'

'Aye, but, what I mean is, you'll grow up, you see, and do things and run about and you'll think that what you're doing is important, but it's not.

'Being alive is important. Everything *else* is a waste of time.

'Sometimes I'll look at the moon and I'll know that she's seen it all before and she'll make me remember what this is about: I'll just be alive for a while and not need to do anything else. You'll be more alive than me, though. Won't you?'

She nodded while he kneeled down into the earth and held her shoulders.

'You'll remember to do that for me. You'll not waste it all, like me.'

'No, I'll not.'

'I've made you sad now.'

'No. No. I'm not sad. I'm thinking.'

She smiled to make him sure that she was happy, with him holding her, looking into her face, just brushing her cheek.

'You ready for your tea now?'

'Aye.'

'What would you like?'

Sometimes even now, when Margaret sees the moon as she goes to sleep, or takes a bath and feels that slipping, comfortable feeling after the first almost pain of relaxation, she is thinking of her father. Without even knowing it, she is stretching her arms up and round him; his sweater is tight against her face, the dip in his ribs is underneath her chin and his heart is beating. There is an atmosphere of Lifebuoy soap, of pruned leaves and of varnish.

In the moment it takes for her eyes to blink as she settles into pillows or warm water, this atmosphere turns through her head and vanishes. Her father and her pleasure have always been close. As if one could not be there without the other.

Margaret is sleeping now.

It is three o'clock in the morning and the sparrows and dunnocks are trying out their songs. Windows along the street have full dawn against them and Margaret Hamilton lies behind the dark of her curtains, asleep.

A week ago, Margaret was still employed and today she is not. Because she was prepared for this, she had her railway ticket ready and this morning she will travel away from here. Probably, she will come back, but this is not certain. She is going away to think about things like that.

Asleep, she is surrounded by waiting. In her kitchen, her half-packed holdall is waiting to be filled, the kettle waits to be boiled and the curtains are waiting to be drawn. In a street a mile away, the sleepy taxi driver who will take Margaret to the station is waiting by a hamburger van with his radio turned off. And away in the city the railway station is expecting her.

At almost exactly seven, Margaret wakes up.

Without an alarm clock or other assistance, this is quite hard to arrange, unless you know the trick of it. Margaret's father taught her how. Just before you fall asleep, when the lights are out and everything else is done, you must hit your head off the pillow, once for each hour of the time when you wish to wake. Margaret hasn't done this since she was a girl. When she was ten, her father bought her an alarm clock to use instead.

But yesterday evening, alarm clock broken, her preparations for sleep sounded quite like this:

PFFUPH, PFFUPH, PFFUPH, PFFUPH, PFFUPH, PFFUPH, . . . PFFUPH.

Or this:

Alright then, seven, it could even be half past, but you can't do halves. At least, I don't think so.
ONE.
And I want to sleep tonight.
　　TWO.
Please.
　　　　THREE.
Train tomorrow. London.
　　　　　FOUR.
God, I'm too tired to sleep.
　　　　　FIVE.
South. Do I really like the English.
　　　　　　SIX.
Who cares? Nobody cares. The English don't bloody care. Sleep, fuckit.
　　　　　　SEVEN.
The English don't *know*, so of course they don't care. I didn't tell them I was coming. I'll have to ask someone to watch the flat. I should have thought of that. No point in just watching, they'd have to come in. I couldn't ask Colin, not now. No nonono no no. Sleep. Everything's fine. Sleep.

Seven o'clock, I'll wake.

Clever Daddy. I wonder how he knew.

And Margaret does sleep and doesn't stir once until almost exactly seven the following morning.

Usually, for a journey, she will dress in something practical like a sweater and maybe jeans. Today, she will put on a suit, as if she were travelling to London for an interview. This is because, in the job she has lost, she was almost always dressed in jeans and sweaters and now she wants a change. Margaret is making a new start and intends to feel different and formal when she and England's capital meet. Also she knows it isn't good to let yourself go when you don't have a job; she's seen what can happen when people do that.

Margaret is wearing perfume; one made new by lack of use. It surrounds her every time she moves and has given her wrists a slightly bitter taste. As the day progresses it will change and fade.

Her taxi arrives a little early and she darts out to sit in the back, feeling odd and not wanting to speak. She is still waking up and the city which passes by her is curiously unconvincing. Buildings like tall, heavy ships swing round about her, shining with glass and blasted sandstone; scaffolding and sails of plastic sheet.

A very few people are out walking, their faces lit by a sky which is the strident blue of plates. Inside the cab, music is playing and Margaret feels; as she sometimes does; that she has inadvertently started to be a film.

As soon as she reaches Central Station, this feeling intensifies. Margaret pays the driver quickly, lifts her bag and leaves the taxi with the kind of smooth and purposeful speed that cameras might expect. Her impetus carries her far into the body of the building before she can recover herself.

The station is nice, she likes it. The period wood-panelling and glass, ripped out several years ago, is slowly being replaced by imitation wood-panelling and glass. The pale, hard floor, beefsteak tomato seats and the more or less garish shop-fronts combine peculiarly as amplified music washes down and a high, black indicator board rolls and pulses hugely. This could be a place of worship.

Over by the photographic booth, two drunks are quietly cutting each other's hair in the mirror provided. People with an air of going to work are running and striding and straggling as Margaret simply walks, but the majority of figures here are still. They are standing like an operatic chorus awaiting revelations from above. Their positioning is beautifully regular, their postures both relaxed and alert, as they gaze at the platform numbers, destinations and arrival times, all crossing the board from nowhere into nowhere, constructed out of tiny yellow squares. The crowd seems very much at peace, very focused, just a little unnerving.

Margaret peers up just enough to see her platform number and is careful not to pause. The train is snug by the platform and while Margaret searches for the carriage labelled H, four policemen take away the barber drunks.

Although there is no one sitting near her, Margaret settles herself quickly and then pretends to fall asleep. No one will talk to her if she's sleeping. Only a ticket inspector will even try.

Margaret hears feet and a distant child and luggage, the traditional whistle blast, and then the tug of movement begins. In a way she does not understand, a murderous electric current pulls her and the carriage out of the station and away.

If she opened her eyes to look out and down the river,

Margaret would see a layering of bridges, stretching east before and then beside and then behind her as her own bridge is crossed. Everything is blue, the sunlight and the water, the sky behind the dark blue bridges and their shiny blue buses and cars. The river always turns its mornings blue.

Margaret settles her head more firmly between the window and her hand and when the horrifying speed of her progress has ceased to alarm her she begins to fall asleep. Before she passes Motherwell, she is dreaming.

From one sleep to another, there she goes.

Late in his life, Margaret's father forgot how to sleep and of all the people who knew this, he was the least concerned.

'It isn't as if I'm still working. It isn't as if I can't nap. I can nap if I want to, any time. If I needed to sleep, I'd be tired, wouldn't I?'

Because no one was with him all of the time, no one knew if he napped. Nobody could be certain, when they saw him, still and with his eyes closed in the easy chair, if he was thinking, or napping, or simply humouring them.

When Margaret came to visit him, he seemed only slightly changed. It seemed there was only a very thin callous of time across the father she had as a child and the one she had now. If she nudged her daddy down beside her on the sofa and they talked, their heads resting back, inclining towards each other, they could have been speaking in any time. If she called through from the kitchen and heard his voice, only his young man's voice, he could have been speaking to her from one of their after-school discussions. They might have been planning an outing, or what she would like for Christmas, bearing in mind that she wouldn't get it, because Christmas should be a surprise.

'Alright, then, what would you like?'

'Nothing.'

'You'd like to have nothing?'

'No.'

'You'd like to have something?'

'No. I *wouldn't* like one of those things that you blow down and press the keys.'

'You mean a saxophone.'

'No. These things are plastic. They sound like a paper and comb would, only better.'

'Mmm. I thought you might hate to have a telescope. Funny.'

'Oh, I'd really hate that. Yes.'

'Good, good. Well, you'll not get that, then. That's a relief. And now.'

He folded his hands round her waist, nearly tickling, but not quite. He bristled his stubble against her cheek, blew on her nose.

'Who do you love? Just out of interest. Anyone?'

'I love you. I love you.'

'Only me?'

'Only you.'

'You're a good girl.'

Their wee catechism.

He would always begin it softly, at the tail end of something else, as if he wasn't sure of what to say. Margaret would always answer twice, to make him sure.

'I love you.' Loud and firmly, a quiet shout, and then, 'I love you.' Softly, to give him all the feeling and stop him being frightened by the shout. This became the only way she could say these words to anyone, although she didn't notice this for some time.

When they had finished speaking, he would touch her head or stroke her face and never be as happy as she hoped.

Margaret was happy with the telescope. It combined things

13

for her pleasantly. She loved the fresh autumn nights near her birthday, their hungry smell and that obscure excitement they made her feel. She loved to disappear into watching, to be nothing but eyes. She loved the peace of doing something by herself. It wasn't like school, or even being home with her father. Two of you couldn't watch; it was impossible for you to see the exact same things. She could look through the one eye of the telescope, the only person there, or needed there, and she could be peaceful and enjoy the night.

She sat in her room while the rows of rooftops and streetlights spread away into shadows and dots; a blush of orange rubbing up beyond the hills. At night, the hills seemed just humps of black nothing, but she knew what they really were. Her light was off and her window opened right up, the door was shut and muffled with her quilt, and she sat in the full feel of the outside and the dark, inside the house and there with her. She watched the colours of the stars and planets and the nothings in between and felt they were lifting her to them. This was the time when the path was opened, when she could choose to walk out from her window and up and into the moon. Asleep, she would dream of running on air. Thin, unscented air.

Her father thought it was too lonely to sit by yourself and look at bright things so far off. He had hoped to be with her, holding her shoulders and giving the little scatters of light their right names, but she didn't want to know what she should call them. She just wanted to watch the stars turning and think of the bigness of distance and of time and then look at the patterns of streets round her house and be sure they could never change.

Deep in the long winter term at school, Margaret would only feel real when the sun had gone down and she was alone by her window, looking up.

In retrospect, her schooling seems absurd.

Margaret's education was in no way remarkable, it merely took the Scottish Method to its logical conclusion, secure in the knowledge that no one would ever complain because, after all, it only affected children.

Margaret, like many others, will take the rest of her life to recover from a process we may summarise thus:

THE SCOTTISH METHOD
(FOR THE PERFECTION OF CHILDREN)

1. Guilt is good.

2. The history, language and culture of Scotland do not exist. If they did, they would be of no importance and might as well not.

3. Masturbation is an abuse of one's self: sexual intercourse, the abuse of one's self by others.

4. The chosen and male shall go forth unto professions while the chosen and female shall be homely, fecund, docile and slightly artistic.

5. Those not chosen shall be cast out into utter darkness, even unto the ranks of Her Majesty's Armed Forces and Industry.

6. Pain and fear will teach us to hurt and petrify ourselves, thus circumventing further public expense.

7. Joy is fleeting, sinful and the forerunner of despair.

8. Life is a series of interwoven ceremonies, etiquettes and forms which we will never understand. We may never trust ourselves to others.

9. God hates us. In word, in thought, in deed we are hateful before God and we may do no greater good than to hate ourselves.

10. Nothing in a country which is nothing, we are only defined by what we are not. Our elders and betters are also nothing: we must remember this makes them bitter and dangerous.

Funny old things, schools. Margaret can easily imagine her headmistress, even now – a piercing, yellow mouth, craned across the black wood of a desk.

'Don't you want to die for your country?'

Margaret couldn't understand the question.

She only remembers standing in a gravel playground each year, each second Friday in September. Rehearsed to the point of hyperventilation, the Pipe Band would advance in long-haired sporrans and white spats. They played 'The Flowers Of The Forest' and 'Scotland The Brave' and the Brownies fainted.

The Brownies always fainted. They would be marched out in close order through the dark of the morning, a full two hours before anyone else, and stood to attention, brown and taut in cotton dresses and knitted hats. The honour of their pack was in the balance.

As the bugler blew the reveille from behind the Domestic Science block, forward came the columns of girls and the columns of boys, all searching for their special marker Brownie. Each column would string itself out behind its Brownie, safe and still. Without the marker, they would have to wander, lost and incorrect, perhaps halting in entirely the wrong place, perhaps never halting at all.

Usually, the Brownies would last until the opening prayer.

Then emotion, the swing of the kilts, or simple exposure would begin to take their toll. By the time Margaret first made her dot in the Armistice Day Photograph, a special team of Brownie bearers had long been a vital element in the display. As the morning progressed, they would lift up their little fallen comrades and carry them away. They had bright faces and stepped in time.

For older members of the staff, the symbolism of these moments would sometimes prove too great. Lowered heads and coughing often hid a tear.

Margaret can't quite describe her school; if she tries, things seem to get away from her. She can't be sure if what she remembers is totally true or not. Her head fills with marching columns and the Twenty-third Psalm and she seems to have always been marching or singing, as if she were in preparation for some kind of war. Over the years, she has invented sequences for effect, but only because the reality makes no sense.

She can shut her eyes and watch a huge, square-headed man gradually take off his jacket to belt a boy. The boy has blond hair and is almost obscenely smaller than the man.

'Sometimes, when I belt a boy, I only take my arm back to here.

'Sometimes, when I belt a boy I lift my arm, right up, as far as it will go.

'Sometimes, when I belt a boy, I take my jacket off.

'For you, boy, I'm going to take my jacket off, then I'm going to roll up my sleeve and then I'm going to make you very, very sorry.'

The horror of it stayed with the class, all day. No one would go near the blond little boy, in case whatever badness he had around him would spread to them.

Such merry brutality soon became commonplace. Margaret smiles as she thinks of the maths teacher, the one with the greasy hair and the uncertain fly, who would beat a boy or two almost every day. The boys responded by spitting, smoking and starting casual fires in their desks. It seemed a natural part of things. For half their time, Margaret and the others would observe themselves like strangers, just to see how far they'd go. The rest of their day, they gave to the fight. It was a way of life they were so used to, they almost believed they'd invented it.

Margaret only realised that she didn't like her school on one of those marching, drizzling Armistice Days. A real Armistice Day with real Brownies. It was that terrible Day when Frazer MacTaggart, the chosen Pipe Major, flung his six-foot ornamented staff high through the layers of rain and then didn't catch it.

Every face in the columns of faces tilted up to watch the staff in flight and suddenly knew that Frazer MacTaggart would miss. The faces turned towards Frazer and made him know. He stuttered only a little in his marching, before the staff point caught him a wheeling blow on the shoulder and he fell.

The rest of the band marched around him, not knowing what else to do, and a group, perhaps of Brownies, ran out to help him away.

Margaret's was the only face that laughed. It wasn't spite, at least she didn't think so, she was simply very happy. Her school would have to be ashamed now. Not her; her school. An act of God had hurt its pride. Clever God.

It was hard for Margaret to tell her father what it was really like out there, away from his home. She didn't know if he could understand. When she came home crying because the lady who taught them sewing had spanked her, she already knew that he wouldn't be able to help. She told him that she couldn't use a thimble because it made her stitches go all wrong and Mrs Parker would shout at you for that, but if you sewed without your thimble, she shouted, too.

Daddy held her on his knees with his nose in her hair and didn't say anything. His breathing felt very hot and she imagined it would make her head less sore, so it did.

'Come on, now. No more crying. You've made my shirt all wet.'

'Sorry.'

'It's alright. It's alright. Here you go.'

She took his huge, fresh handkerchief and wiped her face and he looked at the window, beyond her head.

'We'll have to buy you a thimble and you can practise.'

'I can't do it.'

'If you practise. It's only that you've never used one. Your mother would have had one, I think she did. You have to please these people sometimes, even if they're silly. She's silly. You know that?'

'Mm.'

'Who's silly?'

'She is.'

'Who?'

'Mrs Parker.'

'Mrs Parker is silly. Go on. All together.'

'Mrs Parker is silly.'

To please him, she giggled. Thinking of the chalky fabric smell of Mrs Parker and how she would always win, Margaret giggled. Daddy seemed convinced.

Margaret's father walked her down to the chip shop after that.

They looked at all the other gardens and her daddy's was still the best. Sometimes she wanted to cry again, but she knew that she couldn't outside, because people would see and they would think it was her father's fault. She wondered if he'd known she wouldn't cry outside and that was why they'd come.

That night, she thought she heard him very late, walking about in the living-room by himself.

Probably, Margaret could say the sound of her daddy, up and pacing out the night, had run through her thinking for something like twenty-three years. Through her presence and her absence in his house, it ticked out her worries which were his and his worries which were hers. The space where she expected his sound to be was still unoccupied in her head.

As she dreams in the train, there may be the hush of slipper footsteps, still walking through her mind. Something like her breath or her heartbeat, or the sound of a slow dance step.

One November, Margaret phoned her father. They were both near the end of those twenty-three years they had together. Twenty-three years. As long as a marriage, maybe two.

'How are you?'

'Fine.'

'Are you sleeping?'

'I'm fine, Margaret. Just fine.'

'That's good. You'll be sleeping at night then. That's good. I had thought that, if you weren't sleeping at night, it might be a wee bit boring. I thought you wouldn't like a video recorder. To pass the time. I thought that would be no use to you.'

'They're very expensive.'

'Good thing you don't need one.'

'Too expensive, love.'

'Well, like I say. Anyway, what are you doing with yourself? How's my Daddy these days?'

When the video came, he seemed happy; he bought tapes and hired films from the garage across the street. He read the leaflets on how it worked. If he wanted to record a programme, he had to kneel down and lean on his elbows, then squint at the little green numbers, press little keys. He found that all quite difficult to do. His knees were stiff. And it seemed his fingers were very large for the remote control. The keys were certainly small and close together, so close he would often press two of them at once. The thing was not intended for his size of hand. It was a shame, he would have used it, if he could.

Nobody liked him. Somehow, nobody liked the man. He brought out the childishness in you; almost enjoyed your spite.

When people discussed Mr Lawrence – nice people that Margaret knew and liked – they always seemed to end by simply staring at the round blank he made of his face whenever he passed. His eyes would shine under their hate.

For three years or so, Mr Lawrence was Margaret's employer.

And he always called her Margaret, her private name, the one her father used.

And he always met her eyes when they spoke; felt for them and met them and gave a little kind of push. Nothing obvious.

And he always made the time to give her advice.

'Those young people. Margaret? Listen, those young people. Are they safe?'

'I'm sorry?'

'There's no need to be.' He gave a grin after that. 'No need at all. I'm asking, are those young people you work with safe. You should be careful. The boys, well, they're hardly really boys any more, are they? Should you be with them on your own? Do you know if they drink, take drugs? Someone like that – in that position – could do anything. They don't understand the harm they cause until it's too late.'

'I'm sure they're fine.'

'If you were worried at any time, you would tell me.'

'Yes.'

'I know you're on your own now. I didn't know your father, but . . . one hears things. Please do ask for any help you need.'

'I will. I'm fine.'

He pressed her hand with a snatch of a smile.

'I have to go now, Mr Lawrence.'

'Of course, of course.'

As tall, green barley smears across the windows of her train, Mr Lawrence walks across one of Margaret's dreams. She can feel his breath like dust across her cheek as he whispers to her and moves away, leaving a sour, little space of sadness. Then her mind draws up the smell of hot, small gravel and the feel of it, ground by her feet. There is also the sound of water and children enjoying it. She smells the fall of sunlight across skin and gravel dust. She sees the square, grilled windows and the tired, oblong walls of what everyone once decided to christen the Fun Factory.

This is a memory from the summer. One of the standard, mostly wet summers that came even after the climate began to go wrong. For precisely six days in August the sun would shine and that would call out the paddling pool and the weans, all squeezed on the only available patch of grass, between the chairs dragged round from the café, an Alsatian the size of a horse and the sun-bathing percentage of the unemployed. Nothing much seemed to get done, Margaret ate ice-cream and it was nice, maybe even Fun.

Calling their particular work-place Fun was a simple necessity, because calling it the Community Link Centre (Drop-in Café,

23

leisure, arts, soft seats and welfare advice) seemed to make its borstal windows and its tiredness far too obvious and no one liked to be reminded of the numberless, larger failings it could in no way alleviate. No one liked to feel they were constantly failing and hemmed in.

Counting Margaret, there were three of them at the Factory, having Fun: Sam and Lesley and Maggie. She always liked to be Maggie here.

'Maggie, you know where the chess boards all went?'

'Maggie, that man's in the café again and Sammy isn't here.'

'Maggie, his mammy's just told me the Alsatian's ate wee Sylvester. Is that right?'

It was nice being Maggie. She was a Centre Assistant. This meant, among other things, that she typed and did the filing. No one else knew how to do that, so no one could say it was wrong. She generally got Lesley to do the accounts and sometimes she could just sit and drink a coffee; watch the TV they'd bolted to one wall. Sometimes she allowed herself time for that.

They were all Centre Assistants. Rumours suggested that once there had been a Senior Centre Assistant. The power had gone to his head, it was said, and he hadn't lasted long. Assistants' duties were outlined briefly on photocopied sheets along with their RESPONSIBILITIES. Mr Lawrence was especially fond of them.

'Margaret, I give everybody one of these. I would just like to point out that I personally find the tone of the language quite unpleasant. I want you to know that I don't deal with people like us on these terms. You'll learn about this – I'll teach you – there are different ways of speaking to different people. I'm afraid my priority has to be that I'm understood.'

'Right.'

'Perhaps you could think of a better way to put this. That might be fun. Talk to me about it, sometime.'

'I'll have a think.'

'Good girl.'

He couldn't touch her hand that time because one of them was in her pocket and the other was still holding the sheet.

TO ALL CENTRE ASSISTANTS

REMEMBER the REPUTATION of the CENTRE is in your hands. Although the CENTRE is open to all, ANTISOCIAL BEHAVIOUR, POLITICAL DEBATE and agitation on behalf of DUBIOUS MINORITIES cannot be tolerated. No YOUNG CHILDREN may be left UNATTENDED, no TOOLS, FURNITURE, ELECTRICAL GOODS, PETS, CURTAINS OR LINOLEUM may be stored and under NO CIRCUMSTANCES may CREDIT be extended by the CAFE. CLIENTS are not to be encouraged to linger on the premises without CONSTRUCTIVELY OCCUPYING their time. SINGING, DANCING, FIGHTING, DOMINOES, or OTHER GAMBLING, ALCOHOL, CHIPS, FISHING MAGGOTS and CLIMBING BOOTS are forbidden. As are RELIGIOUS TRACTS of THE ALTERNATIVE kind.

AT ALL TIMES, BE AWARE. YOU ARE RESPONSIBLE.

Margaret wondered what kind of people Assistants were meant to be: Different, or Like Us.

Without further information, each of them did their best. They helped to run the centre, to administer and organise. They were ever alert for religious tracts and rogue minorities and when the petty cash had been counted and the toilet paper bought, each of them could contribute to the Fun.

Lesley specialised in pursuits of the life-threatening kind: her groups abseiled and climbed, white-water canoed and were hoping to parachute. She would only countenance fishing if it took place on unsuitable seas.

Sam was the video expert and photographer. The video had been borrowed, whoever had done the borrowing deciding to do it at night, so nobody knew who to ask to give it back. This loss and the absence of dark-room facilities had driven Sam to his other love, the guitar. He played the guitar very often and quite well, but never showed any sign of giving lessons, of starting a non-singing and non-dancing music group or even just playing free tunes in the café. Margaret considered barring him for not keeping his time constructively occupied. Lesley always wanted to let him stay.

Margaret ran the Young People's Theatre and the Women's Group, until the Women said they'd rather go to College and learn about cake decoration and the maintenance of cars. There was money in that. No offence.

Margaret was disappointed when they said goodbye. She felt useless. She had weeks and weeks of sessions, all prepared, on health and managing debts and assertiveness. It threw Margaret off balance to find that most of the group were already assertive and only in need of a chance to prove it. For a while, she felt people were looking at her in the Centre, because of her unsuccessful group, but that wasn't the case. Only Lawrence ever mentioned it.

'That Women's Thing you used to do, Margaret. Fallen through?'

'We've stopped it for the moment, yes.'

'Exercising their right to change their mind, eh? Seriously. You have to understand that some people here do not know what they want. They say "yes" and "no", but they don't necessarily mean either one at the time. I'm sure you know the•type. You might turn your attention to the café. I feel you could bring something to it. Something special. The right touch. You know.'

Margaret watched him tip-tap away on his shiny segged soles and wondered why she suddenly wanted to wash. She had always tried to think of him as a person. Why did he stand so close to her? Why did he look so sad? What could somebody like Lawrence want? He must be twice her age. And he wore waistcoats.

That morning, a cartoon reeling silently across the television screen and the rooms still cold, she felt she could sit and think about Lawrence, work things out. No one would interrupt her. Bobby The Dug was their first and only customer, so far.

But then something fell and broke in the café kitchen. From behind the hatchway, there came a dull cry.

When Margaret stood in the doorway she saw Heather, the café helper, standing, only moved by her rushes for breath. She was surrounded by peach slices, exploded syrup and curves of glass. Without raising her head from the syrup that streaked her legs, she said, 'I'm sorry. I'm just . . . I don't know what's happening to me. I'm sorry.'

Margaret came back from the Ladies with a sheaf of paper towels, hearing Heather's voice long before she reached the door.

'I feel like it's my fault. It must be my fault. I mean, she's only six, she's just a wee lassie. "I'll batter her cunt in," she says. "I'll batter her effing cunt in." She's six. I've no idea even of who she was talking about – some other wee lassie. Me. She could have been talking about me.'

Heather gathered the glass and peaches, cutting her hands, not using the towels, now hardly seeming to breathe at all.

'I don't speak like that. Not in front of her – I try not to, any time. You have to try. It's the kids round here. It's everything round here – rotten ceilings, rotten windows, dog shite and needles all up your close. Rats.

'Rats.

'You think you're doing right to send her to school, you've got to do that, you think she'll be safe, and she comes back talking like a whore. Just sitting in the grass, out the back with her pals. I check the grass, the grass is alright. Oh God. You have to check everything. Fucking everything. Other people don't do that. They don't have to do that. Other people expect to live as if they're normal.'

She stopped and looked at Margaret as if she were an exhibit or a distant view.

'You'll live like that.

'We should never have come here. We came out to be near my mother and away from him, but he knows where we are, he's found out. My mother's driving me demented. She says it's my fault. Everything's my fault, according to her, but she must be right. It couldn't be anyone else's fault. There's no one else there.'

The two women crouched beside each other, but not together, filling the dustbin with fruit and paper and thick shards of dish. When they had finished the floor was glazed with syrup and spotted a little with blood. Heather drifted into the passage to fetch the mop.

'I'll do it now. I can do it now. That's fine. I'm sorry, I'm all in bits, it's these bloody pills. I'll pay for the peaches.'

'It was an accident.'

'Keep it out of what you pay me.'

'I'll ask Mr Lawrence.'

'You know fine what he'll say.'

Margaret tried a jumpy laugh, but cut it short.

'Your hands are bleeding. Do you want . . .?'

'It doesn't matter. They're a mess in any case. I'm alright now.'

Margaret hovered at the door.

'Thanks for listening.'

Margaret had seen this happen before; she would almost reach a person and then they would get that dark note in their voice, that slight difference. Their face would close with a sharp, wee look and they would push her back beyond their dignity. There would be nothing to do but go away.

The café opened late and Bobby The Dug complained because he never got his tea. Heather just looked at him.

'I can't do this any longer. It isn't working. I've never felt more uncomfortable or unhappy in my life. Never.'

He did look uncomfortable and unhappy. Unwell. She wanted to touch him. To reach. And this was happening at such a ridiculous time – when he had been so reachable, so recently. It was hardly any time since she had danced with him in the ceilidh, fitted her arms round his back and held him in, stomach to stomach, breath to breath. They had moved the way that she and her father never could and Margaret had wanted to be watched, not watching; dancing, not sitting to the side. She had been part of two people, sometimes brushing the other dancers, but always miles above them and away.

Now they couldn't meet each other's eyes. Now everything seemed impossible, particularly being here and now.

'We don't deserve this. I mean, I'm fucking sure I don't. I'm sorry. I've thought about it all night. Longer than that, on and off, but for the whole of tonight. There really isn't a way out. Either we live together, we both commit ourselves, the whole thing, or we call it a day; we don't see each other. Not at all. I am sorry.'

There must be some way to solve this: if they went out and walked, if they kissed. Margaret kept both her hands tight in her lap, silently gripping each other, and it seemed it would be much better to keep them that way. Loose, who knew what your hands could be capable of.

How he could make her so angry, she didn't understand. This didn't have to be a fight, a confrontation. She shouldn't have to offer something up to make him happy, start again. He always wanted to start from scratch, all over again, as if nothing had ever happened between them before. Tiptoe together like strangers, not knowing how far to go. It was ridiculous. It felt like some kind of exam she was meant to be passing.

But it hurt her when he wasn't happy, it felt lonely. His eyes were so pink, straining, looking somewhere beyond her reach.

'It would be nice if you even said something. Will I just go now?'

'No. No, I don't want you to go. I'm sorry. I don't know what to say. I don't know how to say it.'

'Mm hm.'

'I don't. I can't do this. Not here.'

'Here is the only chance you'll get. Christ, I'm not asking you to *do* anything; just make a decision. Are we going to carry on?'

'I'm sorry. I just don't know what to do. I love you.'

He closed his eyes and bent his head a little. She couldn't tell if he was even listening, so she told him again.

'I love you. I do.'

'Fuck, I believe you. I've always believed you the first time. You don't have to say it twice. But I don't think it helps. Margaret? Do you know what I mean?'

'I don't think so. I don't know.'

'Join the club. Join the fucking club.'

Margaret wanted to hold his face in her hands, to slap it, to stroke his cheek. Somehow, she didn't care enough to keep doing this, she could feel it slipping away. When she spoke, she sounded tired.

'I want us to be together. I want to be with you. Nobody else. That's all I know.'

'You wouldn't have any ideas on how we would do that? How we arrange that commitment? No?'

He softened his voice again.

'No. I don't have any ideas, either. I'm stuck, Margaret. You have to help me. If you want this to go on, you have to help me. That's all. Help me.'

Their silence elongated until it was impossible to speak. It was just silly. Margaret wanted to say that it was silly. If, right now, they both realised that and smiled, things would be better. But Margaret couldn't think of how to say it, of how not to cause offence. She had passed the point where useful thoughts could come. This was it over. No one needed to say it – everything had just suddenly passed the point where it ceased to be. Relationship Event Horizon. Zero. Zero. Zero.

Colin crumpled his paper cup.

'I knew this is what I would get. This is your fucking response to everything. Radio fucking silence.'

'I'm sorry.'

'No you're not. If you were sorry, you would do something about it. This is no good. Do you understand me? This is no good.'

Margaret knew there was something she should do, but she didn't feel like doing anything. Zero. Zero. Zero. She watched Colin's mouth as it made his words.

'This is it. I don't want you to phone me, or write or go to places where we'll meet. I'll do the same for you.'

He patted her shoulder on the way out as if she were an elderly relative.

'Take care, love.'

He walked across the road from the café and turned right to cross the bookshop window and she thought how patronising he could be and how nice his hair looked when just a trace of breeze flared through it and let you guess how light it was. There was uneven wear at the heels of his shoes.

It didn't seem at all possible that they would never meet again. Because of this, when a man at a table behind her asked a question, she could answer quite comfortably.

'Yes, that's Colin McCoag.'

She could say that with almost a smile.

'Excuse me, miss. Is that a man by the name of McCoag? Colin, is it?'

'Yes, that's Colin McCoag.'

'I thought that was him. I knew his cousin, see. Small world, eh? His mother was a lovely woman, God bless her.'

Margaret was certain, at that moment, that she knew more about Colin McCoag and the rhythm of his name than anyone else in the world. From now on, that would alter and fade away. The thin-lipped man, who continued to speak and bob his head, could never grasp any of that; not its presence or its pouring away; he couldn't appreciate one part of how she had felt before this and how she would feel after.

Colin's back became a section of a staggering crowd and then vanished altogether. He should be the one she told this to, but now he wasn't here. That seemed unnatural.

The man left her table to step outside, after shaking her hand and giving a farewell bob of his balding head. She couldn't see Colin any longer and, eventually, she couldn't see the man. It seemed everything was leaving her behind.

Margaret stared at the quarter moon and the streetlight through the black, plate glass ahead of her and thought, for some reason, of Susan, a girl who went to school with her.

Susan was a little odd. Margaret would see her smiling to herself from time to time; a peculiar smile, as if she had been looking for something and then found it where she'd thought she would.

Finally, while they poured acid together in the hopes of proving natural laws incorrect, Margaret asked her what she was smiling about.

'Nothing. I'm not.'

The acid affected their fingers where it splashed. Their hands grew a soapy, dead film of skin when they rubbed at them under the tap.

'Now.'

'What?'

'You're doing it right now. You're smiling. You were smiling.'

'So?'

'Why?'

'OK I'll tell you later.'

'Tell me now.'

'I can't now. I'll tell you later. I will.'

'As long as you stop smiling, just now.'

'No. If I stop smiling now, then people will notice. They would suspect. I'll tell you later. OK?'

She didn't see Susan again that day until the bus queue.

'Right, come on, then.'

'You've just jumped the queue.'

'No, I haven't.'

'Aye you have. There's a pensioner behind you, with her

34

umbrella at your neck. Swift and deadly. You know what they're like.'

'I haven't jumped the queue, because I'm taking you back to stand with me.'

'Oh, thanks very much.'

'No problem. Why were you smiling?'

'What?'

'You're not going to get on your bus until you tell me. I'm sorry, but you're not.'

'Oh, fucksake. Alright, but you'll need to come into Burton's doorway – I'm no telling you here.'

Burton's had a useful doorway – sheltering indiscretion and groceries. Proof against both weather and prying eyes. It's not there now.

'Have you ever looked at Mr Foster?'

'Is this it?'

'Nearly. Shut up, will you? Have you ever looked at Mr Foster?'

'That teaches chemistry?'

'Aye, have you ever looked at him.'

'Of course.'

'Really looked?'

'I don't stare at him, if that's what you mean.'

'No, I just mean look. As if he was someone you didn't know. Shush.'

'I wasn't going to say anything.'

'Aye you were. Shut up. If you look at him, as if he was a normal person. You know what I mean – not a chemistry teacher – if you look at him like a *human being*, you can imagine him. Doing it.'

'What?'

'What do you think? It.'

'No, I know that. I mean, are you looking at Foster and thinking of him doing it all the time? In his class?'

'Naow. Not all the time. But once you think about it, you can't help thinking about it. I mean, you can see him, can't you? You can imagine him in bed with somebody. It doesn't seem impossible. Well, does it?'

'Well, no. It doesn't. I suppose.'

'See, now you're thinking about it, too. You can see it, can't you?'

'OK, OK, I can see it. So?'

'So once you do that with Foster. I mean, imagine Foster doing that. You can do it with everyone.'

'If you really wanted to.'

Margaret kicked her schoolbag closer to a dirty pillar and wondered if the people in the shop could hear. If they read lips.

'No, it's brilliant. Think of . . . think of Mrs Blackhead. Right? Right? Can you see her doing it? Slipping off the surgical corsets and the army simmett? I mean you just can't imagine it, can you? It's the same with all the duff ones, you can't imagine them doing it. It's only the human beings you can see. You can only see human beings doing it. I'll bet you. Want to try it?'

'Don't be daft.'

'Chicken.'

'If you've done them all before me, there's no point in me doing it, too.'

'But this is scientific research; we compare notes.'

'Och, alright.'

'Bags I don't get Mrs Blackhead.'

'No, you get Mr Norman.'

'Cow.'

'You're only jealous.'

36

*

Susan and Margaret spent the last three years of their schooling, looking at the staff and the pupils and smiling to themselves. Sometimes they were pleasantly surprised and sometimes they were disappointed, but they persevered. Margaret never found a boy who was a human being, but maybe that was for the best because her father didn't seem to like boys at all. She didn't ever mention them, because she knew it would make him hurt. They didn't talk about it, she just knew.

Although Susan suggested it more than once, Margaret never did their test on her father. Somehow it didn't seem right.

But nobody else was immune. Even now, she hasn't forgotten the technique. Margaret thanks Susan in her head, every time she looks for human beings. When she goes into rooms full of people she doesn't know, it helps her to find out ones that she might like. It helps to ease her nerves and steady her gaze and it will work on anyone: Margaret Thatcher, Myra Hindley, Joseph Stalin, Charlie Manson, Nancy Reagan, Thora Hird. And on and on. She could look at film of the living and portraits of the dead and slowly mark every one of them. Yes or No.

Margaret has often thought, if people tried to apply Susan's test before they voted, what a difference there would be. She imagines that first morning, after the final result; the morning after that day when all the voters couldn't help smiling as they walked into the polls.

Sitting in a pastel blue lecture room in an English university, Margaret tried the test. Only three ladies passed it, and two men. One of the men introduced her to Colin. He told her Colin was Scottish, just like her.

Colin passed the test. She told him that later and he laughed all night.

37

Everybody was certain they'd end up in bed. The only two Scots on an English, English literature course; they ought to form a natural pair. After a while their relationship was assumed and then taken for granted and it must be admitted, they did match very well. Neither of them managed to dress quite like students. They bought second-hand clothes, of course, because new were expensive, but their choices were neither as threadbare nor as stylish as they should have been. There was a formality about them that some of their fellow students found off-putting. Even drunk or stoned, they retained a strange air of propriety. Colin in bars or at social gatherings resembled nothing so much as a thin, plain-clothes policeman or a skinny Mormon out on a spree. Eventually, someone christened him Elder McCoag.

When people got used to him, it was alright. He could laugh in company and skin up in very public places, because he looked far too respectable to ever be rolling a joint. A Scottish upbringing had some good points.

But still, he made Margaret nervous – the things he did. They were things you couldn't get away with. Laws were being tightened round them: there were battles with the miners and then the travellers at Stonehenge. Things were being destroyed, very openly destroyed.

Margaret and Colin graduated in the summer after Orwell's year. They had marched a little, demonstrated, feeling irrelevant; they wanted to make their Woodstock, their Paris barricades, they wanted to believe they could make things alright. Whenever they walked at night, different policemen stopped them and England seemed more and more like a foreign country, even to itself. They began to feel in danger of arrest, of searching, of something undefined.

And of course the drug thing was illegal, you could really be arrested for that; no need for paranoia. But that didn't stop you.

You still carried on. Not because you were freeing your head, all that hippy stuff; if anything it all made your head just a little bit tighter every time, but nobody wanted a free head, anyway. Colin and Margaret simply wanted peace. If you had some peace, now and then, you could manage and they had a chemical peace. Unnatural and therefore guaranteed.

But even that peace could be alarming. That distance it seemed to slide between you and other things. The morning Margaret was woken by her radio alarm, its news broadcast leaking out into her sleep, she seemed to dream of a Brighton Hotel and an explosion. Somewhere in her mind, she heard someone say, 'And Norman Tebbit is being pulled out of the rubble.' And for that tiny moment, she felt very glad.

It worried her later. The way she had just rolled over, still a little high, and been extremely happy about sudden death and injuries. A face she knew showing hurt, being under a building, trapped. Did liking that make her a terrorist?

It worried her when she stood in crowds and heard herself yelling with them, 'One more cut – Thatcher's throat! One more cut – Thatcher's throat!' But she yelled it.

She was even one of the first, on a rainy morning, to leave the shoving policemen, break the crowd and run across muddy grass in the wake of a prime-ministerial Rolls Royce.

Nobody thought they would catch it, but all of them ran. Nobody knew what they would do if they did catch it, but all of them ran. What else was there to do? Stand still and do nothing? Or do something with no point? They did something pointless, they ran.

They had decided they lived in a country where pointless gestures were all they had left to make. There was almost a nobility in that. Ahead, there was an impossible distance to cross – another huge, alarming, unnatural peace that grew out of irrelevance and defeat: dying, unemployment, embarrassing old age. And so they closed their eyes and they ran and danced: irrelevant and defeated. Their gestures were pointless, but glorious. Some days they really believed that. Glorious.

Yet, when students of another generation danced in the streets with office workers until policemen came to clear them away, Margaret didn't dance. When an elderly lady ceased to be at the head of her government and the crown was passed on to a middle-aged man, his top lip like a pink moustache, Margaret didn't dance. Power could have passed to a high-voiced former soldier with a railway junction for a name, or a Welshman with the Tin Man's dimpled nose; she wouldn't have danced. She had become peaceful.

She couldn't dance across that distance, couldn't dance away that deathly fucking peace. But still, she wanted to. Sometimes, like a rise of feeling beneath an antidepressant haze, she would find herself becoming desperate; looking for the possible dance, the step, the move to beat them all.

While Margaret was a student, a first-year had stuck his head through a basement window, cut it almost entirely off, and a friend of a friend had thrown himself from the roof of the science block. Margaret noticed it was possible to die. Even at her age. She noticed despair.

Then the closeness of sadness and dying affected her unpeacefully – it made her in a hurry to get things done.

Margaret lost her virginity in the third week of the second term. To Colin. He took it away to wherever virginity goes.

They undressed with due solemnity, ridiculous in the dark and cramped themselves into a Residency bed. Just before they started, Margaret put her wastepaper bucket out in the hall – the agreed sign. Do not disturb. There are two people in this room and they do not want to be disturbed.

She had never been proud of a bucket before.

Margaret couldn't say why they had chosen then. Looking back, she is certain that it was the right thing to do. It seemed slightly unreal at the time, but not unpleasant and very much the right thing to do. She was in love with him.

The morning before their night, they had their hair cut. They went in, made their appointment and had tea in a tea shop until it was due.

'Why is it cream teas down here are so duff?'

His lips were shiny with tea when he answered her. Shiny and slow and soft.

'Same as everywhere else.'

'No, English cream teas are supposed to be something special.'

'Your father tell you that?'

'Who cares who told me. They should be better.'

'It's Devon and Cornwall you go to for cream teas. This is nearly Birmingham. Who the fuck goes to Birmingham for a cream tea. Do you want a cream tea?'

'No, not so near Birmingham, somebody told me they're duff.'

'Cheeky cow. I suppose we've got to go to Devon now.'

The idea of them going somewhere together made them quiet for a while. It seemed so nice.

In the hairdresser's they smiled and looked daft until they were allowed to sit together. They circled each other's eyes in their mirrors, in reflection, coolly face to face, tousled and a little unfamiliar, very still.

Margaret's hair was long, almost as long as it had been at the very first when she'd asked if her daddy would let her have it cut.

All the way there on the bus, he'd checked with her to see if she was sure. She could always change her mind.

Inside, he'd sat in the corner of the salon, holding a magazine. He was the only man there, in a room full of women who combed and stroked Margaret's hair and told her how sorry she'd be – look how lovely it was. Then they would glance at her father and he would make himself smile.

'She says it's too hot, this weather. Says it's weighing on her brain. I can't persuade her. And it isn't practical for school. It does annoy her.'

'Aw, but it's so bonny.'

'Don't tell me that. I think it's lovely. Don't tell me.'

Walking back with him, so much lighter, she felt slightly ashamed.

'I could always grow it back again.'

'Not if you don't want to, hen. You do like it?'

'Yes, I like it. It's much better like this.'

She'd only said the last bit for badness, but she kissed him to make it up. They took the park way home because Daddy liked the pigeons.

This time, when Margaret's hair was finished, Colin stood behind the little mirror they held to let her see the back. The back looked like the back of something – the way it always does – and then Colin kissed it which made it feel a little different, although it looked the same.

'You seem younger.'

He met her eye in the mirror and then looked away.

'You seem even more respectable.'

'Impossible.'

'Come on, Elder McCoag, I want to do something.'

He met her eye again.

'I beg your pardon.'

'I'm going to pay my bill and then we're going to do something. And I'm not telling you what, except that it isn't that.'

And again. Slowly.

'Oh. Alright, then.'

There was something about him, almost sad.

'I love you. I love you.'

And she squeezed his hand and he looked down into her face.

She took him to the big record shop in town and spoke for a minute to the girl behind the desk, who seemed to find Margaret's accent incomprehensible, but finally she giggled and swivelled away.

And then Margaret gave Colin his piece of Shostakovich and didn't even care if he liked it or not. It wouldn't matter because everything was likeable today.

Speakers at the back of the shop crept out with the beginning of the fourth Ballet Suite and Margaret and Colin walked round inside it, blinded with sound.

'I was going to get her to play that thing from *Witness*. You know, where Harrison Ford dances with the woman up in the barn.'

'Too corny.'

'That's what I thought. This is better.'

'Yes it is.'

The afternoon changed whatever had needed to change, before they would go to bed, do all the usual business and go to sleep.

Their first night was quite loving, very slow, but a little grim. By the time they fell asleep it was still just a tiny bit nervous, still grim. Then at three o'clock in the morning a french horn started playing in the square outside. Lights snapped into the night on all four sides. Some windows opened. The horn playing wasn't good. Whoever was there, in charge of the horn, had trouble keeping his lip and could only remember half a tune.

More lights went on. Colin and Margaret waited while four complete Halls of Residence woke up angry. Around the horn and its player, the silence was very tense.

Colin stuck his head out of the window.

'Listen you fucking drunken English bastard. Play one more fucking note on your fucking horn and I'm gonny come down and disembowel you with it. From the inside out. And there's three hundred people here listening who are gonny want to hear you scream. Bend over, I am on my fucking way.'

The horn player lost his lip, somebody somewhere applauded and the lights scattered out again.

By the time a security guard had arrived and was starting to quarter the square, there wasn't a trace of music to be found and Colin and Margaret had come up from under the covers to get some air.

'Do you think that's me conforming to a national stereotype?'

'Before or after the horn.'

'Come here and say that.'

'I have.'

Their position was no longer grim. A certain distance had been crossed.

Although she has knowledge of what came after it, of other less pleasant things, Margaret can't remember that night sadly. Her first time will always seem good. She cannot repeat it, she is simply entirely contented with the way it was.

Margaret went back to her daddy when her last summer holiday came. Her degree had arrived and the summer was restless. The streets smelt of stale canal water and she just felt very Scottish suddenly, so she went home for a while. Only for a while. Colin said he would miss her and phone her and see her very soon. Take care.

A fortnight on, Margaret got a letter, neatly typed, to say Colin was in London, but would be back in no time at all. He would see her then. He felt they needed to talk. Bye, bye.

A month later and Margaret had returned to their flat in England. She found there was nothing of Colin's there. He had removed himself completely.

She didn't see him again for nearly three years: almost exactly the time she had taken to grow used to him not being there.

'There are few things more satisfying than a compliment directed to one's teeth.

'"You've got nice teeth," they say. Or even, perhaps, "You've always had nice teeth," and at once you feel that unreasonable swell of pride. As if you'd somehow planted them and nourished them yourself, taken an active part in their growth. I don't know about you – I've never lain awake at night and willed my teeth to grow. I can't be praised for that, or anything like it. Maybe that's a fault in me. My teeth are here, in spite of what I do, I don't think about them. Not until somebody points them out.

'I do have good teeth, though. I have very good teeth. Only a little weakness in the gums which can be remedied.

'He's a good dentist, this one. Not bad, in any case. But then, I would say that. He told me I've got good teeth. That's such a lovely, simple thing to hear.

'What do you think?'

Margaret started slightly. She had been standing by the window, hardly listening to the man because his voice had seemed to need no one's attention. Beyond the dentist's initials, painted in black, the depth of the street unfurled in uneasy sunshine.

'Not sure, eh?'

'I don't know. I haven't had that many dentists. To compare him with.'

'Well, there you have a fault in your approach. I carry a constant standard within myself. I could only have seen one dentist in my life and yet I would be quite certain of his worth. I have standards, you see. I always pay attention to my pleasure and my pain. My happiness. It makes life very easy. I always know if I'm enjoying myself. Or not.'

'I see.'

'I knew you would.' The man smiled precisely, with bright teeth. 'My life has been extremely simple, throughout.'

Down on the pavement, patches of water were sparking as they disappeared under heat. On the corner of one block, men were burrowing out the centre of a building. She could see right in.

'You have to control your own life. You must. Think of the alternative. Hm? Work it out.'

He moved to take a seat in the middle of the sofa and for the first time Margaret was aware she was alone with him. Since she'd arrived, she'd been alone with him.

'Of course, there are complications. If, for example, I kill someone, that complicates my quality of life. And I have killed someone.' She watched his hands as they moved above his lap, very neat. 'Now, how am I supposed to deal with that? I have to make a decision. It's just like anything else. I made a decision to kill the man, so I had to follow that through. Anticipate and follow through. Easy.'

She didn't move. It seemed important that she didn't interrupt him. She continued to watch the men in yellow helmets as they worked out pits below the level of the street; far below and hidden by walls laced up in scaffolding. Cars and people could pass, were passing, perhaps believing the building was still there. The walls looked like sandstone, but Margaret could see that behind the facing they were brick and behind the brick there was only air and clay yellow pits. She watched until her eyes began to hurt and breathed as quietly as she could.

'Prisons are not pleasant places. No one sane would want to be inside one. So you must make arrangements to avoid them and that can be done. You avoid policemen and arrest. You have friends. But the fact of the killing can't be denied. I mean the moral fact. Whoever else is punished, for whatever reasons, by whatever powers, I myself must be punished because I am a murderer. A lot of what I believe rests on things like that.

'A problem. Solution? Easy. I punish myself.

'I consider the true nature of my crime. The degree of pain and pleasure I created. My pleasure, his pain, although that need not always be the case. I note the current opinions on crime and punishment, the expressions of public disgust and I decide upon a sentence of eight years. Without remission, effective from the date of malefaction.

'Hard to do. Hard to arrange. I can't lock myself up. I must earn a living, eat, conduct my affairs, but somehow, I must also be imprisoned. It takes thought, but is quite simple in the end.

'I remove my pleasure. Fearless and thorough, I take it all away.'

Hearing the pause in his voice, Margaret glanced round, but the man wasn't looking at her. He had leant back; wiry, grey hands smoothing the hair flat from his forehead, eyes and lips closed. He seemed to stretch, exhaled, then dropped his head forward a little to give her a smile and carry on. She met his eyes and found she could not understand them. They were like blue glass or pottery.

'It was a hard thing to do, it was very hard. For eight years, I

48

lived in this city, dreamed, worked, met men and women, spoke to them, saw and smelled things, spent my money, fucked and ate and ran in the rain and took no pleasure in anything. I promise you, I took no pleasure at all. That's a very tiring thing to do. It makes you fit in places you don't notice, it exercises elements inside you that you cannot recognise. I became a man in training and no one knew it.

'But my time walked on ahead of me then stopped, the eight years gone, and I passed beyond my release; everything changed. I was free. Free in capital letters. Effaredoubleee. FREE. Nobody will ever understand that.

'Nobody knew, when I walked across the square in the peace before lunchtime, the wet earth in the flowerbeds turned an hour before, smelling live and restless, and in front of me, a pigeon lifted, nobody knew why I cried. I sat on one of the benches and I cried. Because of the joy. And the fear, too; at first it can scare you, to know how alive you can be.'

Margaret smiled without noticing it. The man stood up and walked across to the fish tank. He tapped the glass, pushing a space into the water and between the fish.

'Anyway, I'll leave you to it. I can't hang about any longer. Busy life.'

He turned and smiled his white smile which Margaret returned as best she could.

He smoothed his tie into the waistband of his trousers, began to button his overcoat. 'You know the stupid thing? All the time I served my sentence, I fitted in. I seemed to be like everyone I met, I saw what I needed to see and nothing other. Now I can't be comfortable any more, I'm too different. People can't understand the way I see things. That isn't right. That must diminish the pleasure in my life. That must offend against my sense of natural justice. Mustn't it?'

When she had taken her filling and spat out the rinse, Margaret asked her dentist about the man.

'I don't know. It could be Mr Scott. He sometimes waits around when he's had his appointment; he likes to watch the fish. Everyone else ignores them, they're too much of a cliché, I suppose.'

The man is not called Scott and Margaret doesn't meet him again. His name is Webster and in a few months' time he does meet Colin and tells him, among other things, that he has nice teeth.

After the dentist, Margaret walked up the hill. Up and along, up and along, working between the blocks, feeling the city neat around her. She sat on an empty bench in a pedestrian precinct with pigeons beginning to gather about her feet, eyeing for crumbs. She remembered the man in the waiting-room and his flat, blue eyes, wondering if he'd been telling her the truth.

She took a note out of her pocket and read it again. Perhaps for the fifth or the seventh time.

DARLING,

It's a letter from Colin McCoag, who calls her darling. Now and then.

I WANT YOU. RIGHT NOW, I WANT YOU. RIGHT NOW. I WANT TO PUT MY TONGUE IN YOUR MOUTH AND LICK YOUR EARS AND KISS YOUR EYES. I FUCKING WANT YOU.

I WANT MY HAND ON YOUR CUNT. IN YOUR CUNT. I WANT MY ARM IN YOUR CUNT. I WANT ME THERE.

Margaret found this letter at 07:40 today. It was taped across the alarm clock and she had to peel it off to see the time. Now it's almost six – 18:00 – and Colin might be in her house when she gets back because he has a key.

YOU'RE GOING TO GO TO WORK THIS MORNING AND SO AM I. I WON'T BE THERE TO SEE YOU, BECAUSE THIS IS YESTERDAY NIGHT AND I'M GOING AWAY. I DON'T WANT TO GO. I WANT TO WALK BACK TO YOUR BEDROOM AND PULL OFF THE SHEETS AND LOOK. YOU'D WAKE UP WITH MY PRICK IN YOU. YOU WOULDN'T HAVE TIME TO WAKE UP ANY OTHER WAY. BUT I DON'T KNOW HOW MUCH YOU WOULD LIKE THAT SO I'LL ONLY LEAVE THIS NOTE.

WOULD YOU LIKE THAT? ME IN YOU. WOULD YOU LIKE THAT?

I WANT TO HAVE WOKEN UP WITH YOU TODAY. ONCE, EARLY, ROUND ABOUT NOW, AND ONCE BEFORE WE WENT OUT TO WORK.

BUT I'LL SEE YOU TONIGHT. SEE WHAT YOU THINK.

ALSO, I LOVE YOU.

REGARDS, MCCOAG.

She rubs her hand across her cheek. Still numb. Her lips and tongue are thick with anaesthetic and she feels like someone else. Her hand can be impartial, brushing skin that could be a stranger's, because it gives no response. Does she feel like this to Colin? She imagines her fingers are his as she runs them over her lips.

For a while she considers that things can be very unfair. When she sees him she'll want to kiss him, but her mouth won't be working yet. She could end up sucking his nose and know nothing about it. Her mouth will taste of blood and the dust of her teeth.

Not that Colin wouldn't forgive her that, might not even like it, in a way. But for now she remembers how ugly a kiss can feel and that the only kind of kiss she will be making for at least an hour or two will be ugly like that. Her father's kisses became ugly all the time, once his teeth were gone.

Home for Christmas, in her second year at Uni, Margaret met her daddy at the railway station and saw his new face. His mouth was too pink and too white, his cheeks slackened, his lips very cold and a little too wet. Daddy hadn't told her they were going to take his teeth away. He'd never even mentioned deciding to grow old so carelessly.

That night, they hugged a little, before her daddy went to bed. Margaret held on tight, smelling his pullover and soap. She closed her eyes and snuggled in, but they didn't kiss. It seemed they almost never kissed after that. And they never talked about what had happened to his teeth, if it had hurt, or the habit he had of leaving the top set out because they made him gag. There was just less of him now and they had to get used to that.

They got used to most things; for example, the way that Margaret's kisses had also changed. She had grown accustomed to kissing Colin, and, although she didn't often kiss anyone else, she always felt slightly cautious, strange, as if she might do something inappropriate. With aunts and friends and her daddy, she was frightened she might close her eyes and not be sure who she was holding, do something wrong.

When she came back to her father's house, she was frightened somehow. Of what she might say, of what she might shout while she was dreaming, of giving things away at any time. Because, naturally, she kept her news about Colin to herself. This made it her secret, made him belong to her, and if Colin ever left her, she wouldn't have to tell her daddy she'd made a mistake. She wouldn't have the weight of him being angry on her behalf. That was the plan.

As it happened, when Colin did leave her, her father already knew about him and kept any anger to himself.

Margaret did not. She spent long weeks in England, looking for signs; perhaps of him, or perhaps of herself; and being very slowly angry. Hurt. Friends down south were sympathetic, but the final term was over and they were mostly going away, or preparing to go. They were obsessed by the jobs they had or the jobs they couldn't get, or the jobs they were doing instead of jobs: their compromise, their defeat.

Margaret ate her own little defeat. She ran out of money, left England and came home to her daddy again, away from any chance of even seeing Colin by accident; away from London, which was all anybody could tell her when she asked where he had gone.

Back in Scotland, she was angry for months. Then she grew bewildered and lost some weight. People sometimes mistook the confusion in her eyes for stupidity. This also made her angry.

Margaret would walk through hours in the city, to wear out her anger and tire herself enough to sleep. She would pass couples, perhaps kissing or walking hand in hand in the daylight, embracing, tight, and as the streets darkened, things would begin to let go. There were shapes in cars and doorways, short skirts and pale legs outside the nightclubs in town, inside the cafés. Margaret felt herself surrounded by a movement she could not take part in, she was slipping through.

She was a single person when people were always expected in pairs, like eyebrows or like gloves. That was how it seemed to her. She was a single woman when a woman should never be single, but looking for a man, or for the right man, or marrying a man, or living with a man, or thinking about living with or marrying a man, or leading several men a merry dance, or seducing a man, or deserting a man, or trying to understand, reform, divorce, encourage, murder, castrate or like a man. Margaret was single. In the mirror every morning, she looked single.

When Colin came back, he said that he knew what she meant.

'It'll change, though. You've changed since university, so have I. And we were only playing at it then. I know I was, anyway. We have to get used to each other. Then we won't be single. We'll be double – two halfs – I don't know.'

'I'm not going to settle and be a housewife.'

'You mean someone who can dust and iron and cook nice meals.'

'Uh huh.'

'Well, miracles we don't expect.'

'Did I ever mention they always called you McCoag Nae Pals? McCoag the sarcastic pig?'

'You're beautiful when you're abusive.'

'Pervert.'

Sitting within the city, between buildings, on her bench, it was still strange for Margaret to think that Colin was here. She didn't know why he came back and she would have liked to know that. Although it was very nice, just to have him here, she didn't know what would happen, if things would stay this way. She wanted to take him out tonight, right into town where the pubs were, where there were crowds and shouts and men to sell you tomorrow's papers. They could practise being a couple, while everyone else was too busy to notice them.

When she got home she would mention it.

On the way from her bus-stop, almost in sight of the flat, she watched a lime seed falling from its tree, the sunlight caught inside it, making it shine and spin and shine, dropping with unimaginable slowness, so that she had to hold her breath, not blink until it was there on the pavement and ordinary again.

Colin was already there when she got in, her door not locked and the kettle boiling. She told him about the seed and enjoyed it a second time, because he enjoyed it, because people in pairs can reflect each other's joy. It is one of the advantages pairs have.

When Margaret wakes, she is not surprised to find herself still moving. The train has carried Margaret impeccably, never deviating from the track. She reintroduces sunlight to her eyes.

Hers is the final carriage, the one another train would hit if it came up too fast from behind. Margaret doesn't like the very front or the very back of anywhere, they always seem a little dangerous, but here is where her reservation is and long-distance reservations are serious things.

Carlisle Station slips up backwards beside her, grey, almost deserted, under a greyer sky. Rain finally reaches her slowing window. She watches it collide with the glass and imagines the quality of its wetness; most rains, after all, are wet in a similar way.

The train seems to hang by the platform for longer than it should.

Spinning fields of various grain and leaf are again pounding by Margaret's head and speed is obviously being gathered somewhere when the reason for their delay presents itself. Lifted waist high by a staggering guard, a boy appears. A boy or perhaps a man, his face seems older than his body. His hands wave gently and his head rests at a slightly peculiar angle. His face looks anxious, strange.

The guard pauses, briefly checks the reservation and looks

across at Margaret as he lowers the man-boy into the seat beside her. Two women, walking behind, close in with an assortment of cushions and belts, packing them round a body which remains patient, not entirely still. He is arranged like a basket of flowers, a limb display.

'This is James. I hope you don't mind. We have a reservation. We're all going to Warrington, aren't we James?'

James makes a noise which could be 'Yes' or 'No' or 'Maybe' or, 'I hate Warrington and wish never to see it again.' A hand takes hold of Margaret's elbow, its thumb bent round impossibly.

'Don't annoy the lady. It's a long journey, we mustn't annoy each other on the way.' And then to Margaret, 'You won't know we're here. Not really. Hardly at all.'

'It's alright. It's nice to have company.' Margaret wonders if they know she's lying, how long she can wait before going back to sleep. The anxious face turns towards her, 'It's alright.' Two hands are put together, thumbs arching away symmetrically. 'He's saying sorry, aren't you James?' The hands nod and Margaret has to say again, 'It's alright.'

The older of the women, broad-faced, blonde, explores a wicker bag. Four fat marker pens and a notebook emerge with a fold of blank paper. 'There you are, Jamie. You can write about the journey, or draw us a picture. What do you think?' The hands are pushed across the table and return with what they find, the head turns to Margaret, checks her again, mouth working without sound.

'Hello, James.'

'Answer the lady, don't be rude. James can't speak to you, but he can write some things. He has a machine, too, that speaks, but it's awfully noisy. Don't be silly, James, it's far too noisy for the train.'

It takes a long time for James to position the paper just as he wants. The pen top is hard to hold and hard to pull off, the pen is hard to fit inside a fist. To bring the pen to the paper seems to take minutes, Margaret watching, not knowing if she should help.

'James?'

The letters shiver away from his hand.

FUC OF

'I see.'

'Said hello, have you, Jamie?'

'Something like that.'

'Well, just ignore him if he gives you any nonsense. He wants attention.'

The smaller, darker woman dips out into the corridor. 'I'm going to get some tea. That thermos is tainted.' James follows her laboriously with

FUC OF TO

'James?' Margaret waits for the head to turn, 'Anything else to say to me?'

NO

'Uh huh.'

YET

'Uh huh.'

HO

'Uh huh.'

HOOOOOOO

'Oh, Margaret. Sorry. Margaret.'

JAMS OK

'Yes.'

?

'OK.'

OK

Colin liked to talk most on the move. He liked to do things moving. This hadn't been the case before he went away. When they first met it took Margaret several months to get used to Colin's kind of stillness. He could sit sometimes, not blinking, not breathing, muffling his pulse, and she would be frightened that he was dead. Afterwards, she asked him what it felt like and he couldn't tell her, didn't know.

Perhaps the drugs altered his pace. Certainly, you could imagine him throwing something and seeing it curve and fall at half the speed, maybe slower, still under the influence of his hand. His conversations seemed to hover and lose themselves as the spaces between the words ran into silence. Questions could take days to answer, so she didn't ask them. All she could do in the end was interpret his range of quietnesses. To be honest, she couldn't say if they meant a thing.

At least she couldn't complain he annoyed her with snoring. She often woke in the night to find his chest neither rising nor falling, exhaling an absence of breath. But if she touched him, he might speak.

'Hands off McCoag. It's sleeping.'

Whether he woke at these times was uncertain. In the mornings, he never mentioned being disturbed.

Now, he had changed his speed. He was certainly still thin, but now it looked intentional. He trained. There were tracksuits and sweatshirts, plain black, or freckled grey, which might be worn at any time. There were shorts for his running, or working in the gym, and she got used to his smell being altered with the sharpness of frosty grass, of new sweat and swimming pools. Undressed, his muscle pressed beneath his skin, like an anatomist's drawing, or maybe a butcher's chart. He was hard to the touch; soft skin but hardness beneath it.

Outside and dressed he strode along beside her like a very tall dog, conversing on the run, talking down the pavements, discussing through shops. Even indoors, he could be restless, like a child.

'Sit down.'

'What, love?'

'Why don't you sit down.'

'Aye, I was just thinking.'

'Well, take the weight off your brain for a while, you're making me dizzy.'

He walked to the sofa, letting one arm slip behind her as he sat and resting his chin quite gently on her head.

Margaret likes that; that's why it happened.

'Are you comfy now?'

'Uh huh.'

'So what were you thinking about?'

'Och, I was just out this morning, having my wee run, and this auld fella's down by the bridge. He quite often is. I don't think he's a drunk, you know, he doesn't seem like that, he just looks as though he's off his head.

'Sometimes he's curled up sleeping and I wake him when I pass, but usually he's sorting through the papers and the leaves, making them neat. I thought he was saving them up until I watched him throwing a load in the river one time – I think that's what he always does. He stacks everything neatly, then throws it away.

'Anyway, he was there again this morning and his face was covered in blood – fucking big lump out his head, blood in his hair, still running over his eyes. I mean, he didn't seem upset. I stopped in case he was dying or something, but he was just rubbing his shirt sleeve over the blood, then sucking it clean. Over and over. He was speaking. He was saying, "It's me. I can't waste it. It's me. I can't waste it." Out of his mind. Completely.'

'Poor man.'

'I came back from London to get away from that – dafties and weans and beggars all over the street. Lepers and plague carts on the way. And guess what I find up here.'

'Is that really why you came back.'

'No. I wanted to come back. I'd wanted to for months. I knew you were here.'

'How?'

'Somebody told me. I mean, I asked folk and one of them told me. I wanted to be here, I didn't like the atmosphere down there and I did think I might see you. Well, more than that, I hoped, but at least to see you. I did that the first week I got here.'

'I know, you came to the Centre.'

'That was when you saw me. I was there another time. A couple of weeks before that, I followed you home. Lesley and her boyfriend locked up – '

'She doesn't have a boyfriend.'

'Aye she does, wee Sammy. Did you not know? Jesus Christ, you work with them, I thought at least you'd know that.'

'Seriously?'

'Aye, I'll tell you later. So Lesley and Sammy lock up and you're off down the street to choose between the corpy and the deregulated bus. You waited for quite a while.'

'You're guessing.'

'Nope. There was a wee boy at the bus-stop in a red jersey, he asked you for a cigarette and you told him you didn't smoke. You looked thinner than I thought you would and you were tired.'

'I don't know if I like you watching me.'

'I do it all the time.'

'But I know about it now.'

'I only ever do it to make sure you're safe. And because you look nice. Give us a kiss.'

Margaret gave him a kiss.

'And let's dance.'

'What?'

'Dance with me, Maggie. Go on.'

'I don't think I've got any music we could dance to.'

'No, no, no. What we do – I hold you, like this. Waltz position. Mm hm?'

'I'm still here.'

'That's good. I'd hate it to be someone else. Because now we lie down and we dance. No music.'

They steered each other towards the sofa.

'I don't think this is called dancing. I think dancing is something different.'

'We can try it your way next time.'

That was faster, too: like being approached by a bulldozer, a hard mind. Margaret thought she might prefer it slow.

The evening after she came home from the dentist, Margaret asked Colin again.

'Why did you come back?'

'Hm?'

They were almost sleeping, neat in her bed together, a good fit. His head had been lying across her arm just long enough to make it sore.

'Why did you come back?'

'I'm not back, yet, I'm still catching my breath.'

'Not just now; then.'

'Hm hm, mm hm, huh.'

He gave a little cough that moved them both and then turned to face her.

'Why I came back? From London?'

'Uh huh.'

'I wanted to see you again.'

'And.'

'Why should there be an "and"? Why should there have to be an "and"? Are you not worth coming back for, all by yourself? Or do I lie to you so often that you can't believe me when I say that I came back for you?'

'Alright.'

'No, it's not alright. I came back because of you. I've tried every way I can to prove it. I can't do anything else.

'It wasn't great in London and I'll admit, I didn't like it there, but it wasn't all that bad, either. I ended up lodging with my Uncle Archie and he sorted me out. He ran a fish shop. "You canny be a useless dope fiend and work in a fish shop." That's what he said. At least, that's what he said to me. Personally, I still reckon it's the only way to do it and stay sane. Archie was entirely off his head – all that radiation and raw sewage, to say nothing of the actual fish. But it could have been worse and there wasn't anywhere else that I could go. You think it's hard to find a place to live up here? A nice wee job in the city? Down there it was impossible. Everything was impossible. There was nowhere I could go. There was no one I could be with that didn't mean trouble.

'I had to stay with Archie and he did a lot for me. He spoke to my mother and I saw her before she died – we made friends again. Archie even offered to leave me his wee fish shop, to make me a partner. I said I was coming back here. He told me I was crazy. "I'll go anywhere you like for any reason, but I'll not move a half an inch for a woman. Not me. I've the smell of them every day at my work and that's more than enough." That's what he said.'

'I'm glad you came.'

'Are you really.'

'Yes.'

'OK.'

Margaret didn't like it when they argued in bed. You were meant to be peaceful and nice to each other in bed.

It was also the place where they slept.

'Colin? McCoag?'

Margaret's voice seems louder in the dark.

'Mm hm.'

'Colin?'

'Awwff. I'm no gonny get any sleep tonight, am I?'

'Don't be cross.'

'I'm not. I'm fucking tired, it's some ridiculous time of the night, in fact it's in the morning, and I want to be asleep. I asked if I could sleep with you. I know that involves a wee bit of staying awake as well, but I would like to sleep. At least try to. Or how about molesting my body instead of my mind.'

'I just wanted to tell you something.'

'Is it something exciting?'

'Come here a minute.'

He reaches to touch her face.

'What's wrong, love?'

'Come here.'

Margaret fits her head against Colin's shoulder, feels his hand curl round to rest along her waist. She's always thought he does that very well.

'What is it?'

'I just wanted to say I'm glad you're here. I mean here in general. Not just in bed.'

'I'm not going to go away. Unless you want me to.'

'I don't want you to.'

'Good. I'm going to sleep, now. Night, night.'

Margaret lies in the thick of the dark and thinks of something she cannot tell Colin, something she cannot explain which sometimes wakes her in the night, like a cry springing up from out of clear water.

She was in her room. Twenty-one years old, newly graduated, and reading in bed with the little brown lamp on; the little brown lamp that Margaret chose to take away with her to England; the old lamp she has slept beside, on and off, for a decade or more. The lamp lit what she remembers and cannot say, because it is probably unsayable.

She was reading a book she had borrowed from her father, because most of her books were still in England and she couldn't go to sleep without reading, at least for a while.

When a knock came at the door, she had almost forgotten which house she was in, was almost unsure of the country around her. Her father's face seemed surprising as it edged round the door.

'I'm sorry, Margaret, I've surprised you.'

'No. No, it's fine.'

'Can I sit on the bed?'

'You always used to.'

'Well, you're bigger now. I have to ask.'

They were quiet for a while, until Margaret brushed the back of his hand.

'Mm hm, well, you see, I was thinking about what you said at dinner, there. About going back down south and I thought you might, maybe put it off. There are some nice wee jobs going up here, I've been looking for you. I mean, you'll be staying up here, in the end. You should probably have my room now – it's bigger and you'll make it the way you'd like. We'll sort it out. Don't worry.'

'I need to go back down.'

'Of course, you'll have friends and – You'll soon make friends up here again. I see that Susan and Barbara quite often. Remember, from school? They ask about you.'

'Dad. Look, I might not come back. At least, I will come back, but not to stay. I'll probably live down there.'

'No.'

'Some of us have got a flat together. It's very nice. You could visit me.'

'No.'

'Dad.'

'You never told me.'

'Well, I'm still not sure.'

'What's he called?'

'No, it's not like that.'

'I knew there was someone, but I thought you would have told me, I thought I must be wrong, because you would have said. You didn't say.'

'Dad. I would have told you if it was serious.'

'He's not touched you.'

'Dad.'

'Don't tell me he's touched you. I don't want to know if he's touched you.'

'It's alright, you'd like him.'

She felt his hand tightening round hers, the skin smoothed with age. Strong bone. His voice was very soft when he spoke again and he didn't look at her.

'Please don't go. Just don't leave me. Please. Please. Margaret, please. I can't – I was waiting for you to come back. Please.'

He fluttered his free hand towards the lamp and she turned it off. She let him cry in the dark. When she held him, she could feel him trying to pull in breath and his tears on her neck, just below her ear and running down. When he spoke, she felt that, too, as the sound moved in his throat and chest.

'Please. You were always such a good girl. If you leave me, I don't know what I'll do. I can't bear it. Your mother went away. She never came back. You'll never come back.'

His breath flailed out again.

'Of course I'll come back. Silly. I'll come back. Mum can't come back – she died. I love *you*. I still love you.'

'She didn't die, she fucking left me. Did you think I would tell you that? Your mother was a fucking slut? She ran away the first chance she got because I was no bloody good? She might as well have died. Leaving her baby. Leaving me. You're like her, you know that, you always were like her. I knew it.'

'I love you, Daddy, I love you.'

There seemed to be an absolute silence, Margaret couldn't say for how long. And then her father breathed, spoke.

'Don't cling to me. You don't need to cling to me. I know where I am now. I know just where I am.'

He pulled her away, but she lifted her hands to his head, gripped it, held it still, and kissed him. He stopped moving.

'I'm fine, Margaret. You go to sleep, now. I'm fine.'

He touched her shoulder and then stood up from the bed. All she saw was the block of light when he opened the door and the dark shape he made. She didn't sleep.

In the morning, he called her down for breakfast in the way that he always had and they ate in silence, while their plates and cutlery battered and scraped.

Then, 'Margaret, I'm sorry. I say things that I don't mean, I'm getting old. Forget what I said about your mother, she did the best she could and I never should have told you otherwise.'

'It's alright.'

'No. It's not. Finish your tea. We should go to the shops this morning, buy you some clothes. You'll want to look nice when you go back south.'

'Dad.'

'I know, I know.'

But Colin had gone to London and that was that. Margaret had to come home again and explain. Her daddy was sympathetic. She knew he was also pleased.

'I'm sorry. I am sorry. If he's for you, he'll come back. If he's not there'll be someone else. You're very pretty – you'll be able to pick a nice one. Come on, don't be sad.'

'I can't help it. What do you want me to do?'

'Don't make yourself alone. No one has to be like that. It's not a good habit to have, love. Don't be alone.'

He hugged her, gave her that silence again. The one that happened sometimes when they touched.

WATCH THIS

James shivers and scrunches his fingers, lets out a smile. He is about to enjoy himself. He begins to eat his Snowball, not entirely carefully, and Snowballs should always be eaten with great care.

Almost five minutes pass before anyone speaks.

'James Watt, you will never, ever be given one of those things again. That was a treat. And now you've spoiled it.'

James shrugs his hands. A few more fragments of coconut fall and stick to the table-top.

'James, this is ridiculous. That is enough. I'm sorry, he's perfectly capable of eating like anyone else. He just isn't trying. Irene, I'm sorry, hen.'

'There's no need to be sorry. He's disgusting, that's all. You're disgusting.' Irene lurches up with the movement of the train, wiping her mouth with a thin, white hand. James is quiet, looking at her face. 'I'm going to get some paper and then I'm going to sit in the buffet car.' The three still at the table watch her sway along the aisle, her dark hair clipped like a boy's and barely touching the collar of a bottle green cardigan. Margaret thinks how young she would look, if you couldn't see her face. She must have an old face.

'I'm sorry, dear, Irene's always been highly strung. She was – she was disappointed. Wanted a girl, you see. And the other thing, of course. The man just upped and left her. His father. Just upped and left. She says things she doesn't mean, sometimes. Doesn't she, James.'

James holds his hands out carefully to be cleaned, waits for the flannel to wipe his face and dab the flecks of marshmallow from his sweatshirt. Mainly, he just shuts his eyes.

'That's a good man, James, good man. Be patient for your Auntie May. That's right.' May kisses him very quickly on the cheek before Irene returns with some toilet-roll and starts to wipe the table clean. She doesn't speak, takes her purse from her handbag and leaves again.

'Do you know dear, I don't think the buffet car will be open yet and that will be another upset for everyone. James likes you and he's fine on his own, just fine. You wouldn't mind sitting here with him for a while? He doesn't take fits.'

'Um, no, that's alright.'

'I'll not be long. Be good James, there's a man. You're such a plaster sometimes, I don't know.'

James and Margaret are quiet a little. He drags some paper under his hands and then wipes his eyes.

HI

'Hi.'

FUCIT

'What do you mean?'

FUCIT

'Why did you wind them up?'

FEDUP

'Are you fed up now?'

YES

'What do you want to do? Is there anything you want to do?'

NO

'Sure? Why are you going south?'

DON KNOW   DON WANT TO   STAY
GLASGOW   I HAVE FRIENDS

'I'm sorry. I don't want to go, either, but I have to. I could tell you why. You want to know why, do you?'

NO

'You could always plaster instead.' James gave her a look. Slowly. 'It's alright, I didn't mean it. I didn't mean it. James Watt wasn't a plasterer anyway, was he? Eh? He was an inventor, you know that?'

YES   COURSE   NOT A KID   STEAM

'Sorry. I should have know you'd know. Is that why they called you James?'

DON KNOW.

'Let me tell you why I'm going south, going right down the line. Take your mind off things.'

NO

'Sure?'

NO   TIRED   TANKS   THANKS

And he pushes the papers away, lets his eyes close.

'I hope you don't snore, James Watt.'

James waves a hand and smiles, but nothing more, and Margaret turns to look out of the window.

The hills are growing into mountains beneath thickening rain. Tall gates with little bells along their crossbars whirl beside the track; if you can fit your lorry beneath the bells you'll be safe to go under the power lines that are racked across the moors. The bells save your life. Margaret travels too fast to hear if the bells ring when the rain hits them, or if they swing in the wind. Into her mind comes, 'Saved by the bell,' and almost before she hears it, she is thinking of something else.

James Watt dozes, knowing he shares his name with a leading Industrial Revolutionary – a man of steam who disapproved of trains.

Margaret watches the black jets peel around the mountains, on exercise. She does not like them. They have the shape of gliding hands; palms down and fingers stretching forward, thumbs tucked in. The hands go in pairs, in three-dimensional black, pushing paler shadows into the heather and the grass. Margaret wonders if the grass they touch turns yellow, or the heather dies.

To keep her mind from the aircraft, she turns to look at James, considers what she would have told him about her journey, if he had wanted to hear. She isn't sure she understands her story, but she might have if she explained it to somebody else. That might have been useful.

Even now, it seems so unclear. Why she is leaving Glasgow and possibly staying away; there must be a reason for that. Not the ceilidh. Not what happened there. It must have been something before or after the ceilidh; something which happened or failed to happen and now is pushing her away from home.

It seems to have begun with a man called Graham nipping his cigarette out and saying this:

'I fully believe that fish have souls.'

Some around the table will later learn that he made a note of this sentence, and others he will say, in the course of several bus journeys during that week. For now, he will be as impressive and spontaneous as he intends.

'I believe all fish have souls and all feel pain. I believe that when I pull them with my hooks up on to land, where I let them drown, they suffer anguish, terror and the pain of death. When they fight me as I play them, they are fighting for life, when they twitch on the bank and they are dying, it may well be that the sound of their grief goes back into the water, that they cry out in a way I cannot hear. They may even mention my name. It is a serious thing, to catch fish. I do not take it lightly.'

Margaret looked round the room, at Graham's wife and John from the fishing club; two mountaineers, Lesley, Sam, Heather from the canteen, Mr Lawrence and their local councillor. Only the rising tissues of cigarette smoke moved, everything else was still for Graham. Mr Lawrence stared at him and through him and into the far wall behind. Graham didn't seem to notice.

'But I also believe that men have souls and by that I mean human beings of every sort. For the good of our souls, we must eat and find things to do; work with companionship and meaning.

'I kill fish for the good of my soul. I fish with my wife and we provide ourselves with food. My children, and others of our acquaintance, are familiar with trout. The children of the unemployed, more than any others, should know the taste of salmon, or brown and rainbow trout. In fishing, I find the work I am unable to find elsewhere; in fishing, I am the laird and not the ghillie.

'Our fishing club takes families up into places which are good, where they can picnic, walk and run. We hire coaches, we lend rods, we tie flies and buy bait. These things cost money and yet we have never asked this Centre for money. Our club is quiet and law-abiding, it brings custom in, has a varied and numerous membership. All we ask for now is the use of your Centre one Friday night, for a fund-raising ceilidh. We will pay you a hire fee, if you wish.

'We ask this for the good of our children's souls.'

People wondered if they should clap and Heather got up to go to the kitchen. She preferred to sit in there when they had evening meetings – it meant she could read her book and get a wee bit peace.

As she would often say, 'The trouble with folk here is, they can't see there's any difference between volunteers and slaves. Sure, neither of them gets paid.'

The arguments continued: there were good points to be made about bars and glasses, the number of sinks and fire exits, if hot food would be served. Was an important precedent being set: the ceilidh would involve singing and dancing, drink and forms of gambling, would it not? Would children be present? Would a sectarian element creep in? Would ashtrays be stolen, or provided?

Mr Lawrence waited to take the last word.

'Well, I think we've probably spent enough time on Mr . . . Mr . . . Graham's idea. This committee was, you will remember, only formed as a courtesy to Centre users, to keep them informed of our plans. It has no executive power. However, as Councillor Naylor and myself were discussing the possibility of hiring the Centre out to appropriate groups at commercial rates, it may be that the ceilidh will serve us as a useful dry run. We certainly cannot ignore such strong, almost religious fervour on Mr . . . Graham's part. No indeed.

'Perhaps Margaret can see to all the necessary details. Is there any other business, good, meeting adjourned.'

As Margaret locked the final padlock on to the door, Lawrence came back from his car, across the dark gravel.

'Margaret, you don't understand, do you. I can't have decisions forced on me like that. There's a principle here. We take the decisions, Margaret, we make them. That's our job.

'It is also your job to prevent gentlemen like Graham from overstepping the mark. I know his type, you see – scuttling off to Adult Education, getting degrees by correspondence course. I know him, you don't. He can't face reality; none of them can. He can't learn from experience. Believe me, his kind can do nothing but harm. They think their little spark of education can save the world. But how do they save us all? By keeping their wonderful knowledge to themselves. They get what they want and go – leave us behind. He will never change one thing in his life; these people just manufacture dissatisfaction which you and I then have to deal with. Talking about his soul when you can guarantee he doesn't believe in God. We deserve better than him. You and I, we make ourselves useful. We serve the public. We help.

'People want to be happy, that's all. They don't want stupid promises, they don't want to think. You may not like me – people often don't – but I do the thinking for people and I never make promises I can't keep. This Centre is here because of me – so is your job. No one remembers it, but I do provide that little public service for you. Every day.'

He coughed neatly and caught her eye, left a soft pause, smiled.

'Sorry to have to lecture, but I'm disappointed. I interviewed you for this job. And I hired you, picked you out, because of what I knew you could do. You have potential. Take my advice, my friendly advice.'

Another smile.

'Keep Graham and people like him out of your life, or they'll make you regret it. You're a clever girl. You know what I mean. It's not as if you really belong here, is it? It'll be onward and upward for you. Better things.'

Lawrence squeezed her hand before he walked away.

'And there's better company you could keep.'

'What?'

'If you needed a good friend, someone to come to, I'd be there. Do you understand?'

'I – '

'Goodnight.'

'I wish I'd been there.'

Colin made her tea when she got home, took off her shoes and rubbed her feet.

'This always worked with my mother.'

'Thanks. Thanks, love. But I'm glad you weren't there.'

'I wouldn't have done anything. Only gubbed him, dirty old man. Just a wee gub.'

'Exactly. It's not that I might not have done that myself. It's complicated. And I need the job.'

'Nobody needs a job like that.'

'You know how many applicants there were for my post? One hundred. I bet more than half of them had degrees.'

'And the other half would have been qualified for the job.'

'I'm qualified for it, thank you. It's just impossible to work with people in the community, if your boss hates people and communities are being phased out as barriers to enterprise and foreign travel. I thought Lawrence hated me – the alternative is even less pleasant.'

'You'll tell me if he tries anything.'

'He won't. It's probably just a feeling I got. It's probably nothing.'

'Whatever he does, tell me. Only let's not talk about it now, let's take our minds off that. You should look for something else, but not now. You shouldn't look for something else now.'

He slipped his hand under her sweater, already knowing the way. The other hand reached round to pull her close.

'I smell of smoke.'

'That's alright, I taste of whisky.'

'I thought you were in training.'

'Night off.' He licked her eyes, then fed his tongue between her teeth. The whisky bitterness faded, while their mouths looked for something together.

He was good at taking off her clothes now, good at fiddly bras and awkward zips. He didn't give her time to think, just drove on. She folded her arms round the back of his neck while he suckled in, his hands cold against her back. She started to kiss his hair, knowing things had begun and wouldn't finish for quite a while. Colin was changing under her lips, the way he always did. He became almost a boy and quite like an animal, or perhaps a blinded man.

When her father had been with her mother, had he changed like that? Margaret didn't think she changed at all, but wasn't sure if Colin noticed. He never mentioned she was doing something wrong.

They walked to her bedroom naked, bumping elbows and hips, unable to fit through the doorway arm in arm. Margaret stepped through first, oddly modest as she swung into bed; knees together, head low, leaving the sheet back and sliding across to give Colin room.

'You put fresh sheets on.'

'They're not fresh, they're new. I bought them. Some housewife. Did you know you only had two pairs of sheets.'

'What colour are these?'

'They're purple. Can't you tell they're purple. They feel it. You feel pink. Wet and pink, can I get in there, I want to get in there. Get in you in purple sheets. There we go, there we go. There.'

She did like it there. She liked their stomachs being together and their arms round each other's backs. But she didn't know why she liked it, she didn't know why her mind would sometimes wander when they lay together afterwards. Even with him still inside and twitching like a sleepy fish, there had been times when she forgot that he was there.

Margaret hoped she would come tonight. It made him pleased when she did, he would kiss her forehead and stroke her cheeks and he would smile. She never liked to lie about it. Even though it did seem kinder.

'Maggie, Maggie. I'll take you up to the Centre, we'll go up at night, you've got keys, we'll go in and lock the door on the inside and fuck, in the wee front office, we'll do it there, take your knickers off, take off your skirt, and up against the fridge in the kitchen, how about that, with your arse against the fridge, and then we'll go in Lawrence's office, I'll sit in his chair and you can suck me off, taste yourself on my prick in his office, you can sit on his desk and I'll play with your tits and we'll fuck on his desk, me inside you, naked in his office, on his desk, I will shoot my load right up you on his desk.'

Margaret came.

The next morning Lawrence stood in his office doorway and called her in.

'Margaret. I'll expect you to arrange this ceilidh: you'll be *au fait* with all the details: special licence, informing the police, ensuring the entertainment is suitable . . . But if you need any help, I will be on hand. Mmm? Well, I have nothing more to say. Do you? Is there something you'd like to say?'

She shook her head.

'I see. My wife and I, we'll be attending. I think you should meet. My wife.'

Lawrence seemed to be wincing, then he let out a breath and told Margaret she could go. Conversation round the café tables dimmed a touch, Lawrence's door snapped shut behind Margaret's back and somebody somewhere sighed. A match scratched into life, things relaxed.

'The auld bastard nipping your head?'

Heather was leaning over the café counter in her Mother Confessor position.

'How d'ye guess. Could I have a coffee and a wee glass of paraquat.'

'He'd drink it, then eat the glass. Would you like a Penguin on the house, or a custard cream?'

'No thanks, I couldn't take it.'

'Aye, he makes me sick, too. Still, we're getting the ceilidh.'

'How do you know?'

'I heard Graham rehearsing his speech in the gents' yesterday. And wee Hughie said, just now.'

'It'll be more work for you.'

'Oh no, the boys want a ceilidh, the boys can do the work. I'll be there to eye the talent and that's all. Not a tea-bag will I lift.'

'Nae change there, then, eh?' Graham slapped his mug on to the counter.

'Were you wanting that filled.'

'Aye, darling.'

'Well you know what you can do then, don't you?'

'Of course, I shall creep through to the wee man's office, puncture his jugular vein, insert my spiggot and drink his chilly blood at my leisure. Gie's my mug back.'

'I think I'll leave you to it, Heather.'

'I'll just tell him you've ate the last Penguin, then watch him greet.'

'Aw, Heather, man, don't be like that. Hey, Maggie, by the way, we'll deal with the ceilidh and that, don't worry. It'll be a good night.'

'Lawrence says he's coming, you know, and his wife.'

'Jesus, Marx and Lenin, that's the bar in the black.'

'How do you mean?'

'It's thirsty work, being Mrs L. That's why she doesn't get out much – a popular local figure like William Lawrence appearing with a partner who terminates every outing by spewing her ring. If we're lucky. No, no, wouldn't do at all. If Dirty Daisy's coming, we're in for a rare wee time. Terrific.'

Graham winked, touched Margaret's shoulder, saw her walk up the passage that led to the toilets and turn in.

She waited until she was sitting, the cubicle door snibbed shut, and then leaned her head forward, into her hands, ready to cry. It didn't come at first, because she had held it back for just too long, but then she felt the tears against her palms and a rising sob.

When she had finished, she seemed chilled and her throat was aching. She ran the tap and held handfuls of cold water up to her face, drinking some and shivering. There was no mirror so she couldn't tell how she looked. But she knew it would be bad.

The Youth Theatre wanted to do something in the ceilidh.

'Can we?'

'Hm?'

Tam took Margaret by surprise, slipping up behind her shoulder, the way that he usually did.

'Can we do something – in the ceilidh?'

'I wouldn't have thought you'd be interested in a ceilidh.'

'We're not, it'll be pathetic – but if we do something, folk'll come.'

'Aye, we could get loads of people to come.'

Margaret found herself in the mouth of a crowd.

'What kind of people? The Drugs Squad.'

'Actually, we could get loads of folk and our teachers – half of them are old hippies, anyway, they'd think it was great.'

'Wee Chrissy could bring all her social workers. Fill the place.'

'And you could bring all your customers.'

'Spin on it, slag.'

'Get tae fuck.'

Margaret likes the Youth Theatre. They somehow understand each other. She goes to their rehearsals and feels herself relax while they do her swearing for her, run and fight, while they talk about Mr Lawrence in terms she feels it would be unprofessional, if not unwise for her to use. They're Fun. Gus, Elaine and Susan, all the rest, they all have something Margaret would like: a kind of insolent relaxation, a pride. It's an attitude she wants to learn about.

'What would you do in the ceilidh, Gus?'

'What everyone else does, Auntie Maggie, we'd fucking sing.'

'If we came here to practise every night, we'd do it no bother.'

'Tam, the last time we tried to do that much rehearsal, you all ended up barred. I think you might still be barred.'

'We wanted to be barred, then. This time we don't.'

'Well, thanks for explaining that. I was finding it hard to understand. Once you get to my age, the senility creeps in.'

'Naw, it's just your sinful life. We'll come straight in from school. Four o'clock.'

'Aye, four o'clock.'

'And we'll practise for the gig.'

'How many nights?'

'Every night.'

'Naw. We'll have Mondays and Fridays off.'

'Why can't we come on Mondays.'

'Well Susan can come any time, but. Can't you, eh?'

'How would you know, prick?'

'The BB marching band told me. All thirty-four of them.'

'Couldnae get it up without a splint, you're fucking jealous, Gus.'

Margaret knew they would get things decided in the end and she had learned to keep very calm and wait. The Youth Theatre wouldn't understand impatience in anyone, on principle.

*

'Shut up. So. Right. We'll start next week. Next Tuesday. Maggie can you come every night.'

'No comment, eh, Auntie Mags?'

'I can be here most nights, but I do need to go home sometimes.'

'So do we.'

'Aye, but she's got a man to go to.'

'Aye, Colin. I've seen him. Nice arse.'

'I go home to have my dinner, watch the telly and go to sleep. The things that normal people do, you know? And talking of which, it's time to go home now; past time and I'm starving.'

'Aye, but there's no a janny here. We don't have to go.'

'I'm the janny. Come on and get lost, or I'll lock you in.'

'YEEEES!

'Lights going off now, burglar alarm going on – you've got two minutes. One minute and fifty-eight seconds, fifty-seven . . .'

The Youth Theatre evaporated, whooping into the night, banging the grilles across the windows and trailing wolf howls. They prided themselves on being predictable. Except when they weren't.

Gus, whose proper name was Raymond, had just lost his Saturday job in the supermarket. He'd stolen an old stuffed weasel from the art room at his school and hidden it under the sausages in the fresh meat display.

Gus had slowly unravelled a layer of pork and beef links and a nice wee lady customer had obligingly collapsed. She had glanced down at two little glinty black eyes and a long, long weasel tail and then passed out.

Nobody knew why he'd done it, not even Gus. It wasn't as if he didn't need the job, or at least the money from the job. But the look on the nice lady's face as she slipped down the counter, the easy way the weasel lounged against the sausage meat; he found that all very pleasing, very pleasing indeed. Even when his father punched him for being an arsehole, Gus felt pleased.

Margaret rode the bus home, still thinking of Gus, of how he was able to do something like that. She had only ever been rebellious as an infant.

Her baby memories are full of startling wilfulness. She looked up at the sky through the square mouth of her pram and saw a bordered world, the same shape of world where spaghetti westerns happened. Cinemascope. Perhaps for this reason she glared at everything outside her like a tiny gunfighter; belligerent, uncontrolled and perversely endearing.

She still finds trips to the cinema strangely comforting, but in her pram, the sky beyond her had always been very bright, more white than blue, and she much preferred to lie on her stomach and look at the dark.

She seemed to have been born set in her ways. In harsh weather, she wanted to be without shoes and gloves and socks. She would squirm them off, only to have them replaced for fear of coldness. She would cry and start to squirm again. Margaret would lie on her stomach, and not on her back, so her father would faithfully change her about, for fear of her smothering. She would rather dangle, upside down, from the slope of her father's lap, something forbidden, for fear of her eyes being turned. She would worm to the edge of his knees, like a little seal, until her head hung in mid-air. She had a photograph of herself in just such a position.

Margaret worried her daddy, by being so strange when he was just a man and wasn't sure what he should do about it. Women he hardly knew would give him advice in shops and on street corners which made him sure he was failing as a father: his faults must be so obvious.

As Margaret grew, her character seemed to shrink and by the time she was Gus's age she had almost forgotten what she was like. And, oddly enough, Mr Lawrence and the Factory were proving very educational.

'Graham?'

Margaret caught him in the café, eating two potato scones with cheese. The house speciality.

'Aye, hen, don't fret. We've hired the stripper from a feminist collective and she'll jump out the haggis, with a carbon rod in each hand, just as we finish singing "Dainty Davie". How does that suit you?'

'What?'

'You were wanting to talk about the ceilidh. See how things were gaun?'

'Well, yes, but really I wanted to tell you about some participants. If that's alright.'

'You can sing anything you like. As long as it's passed by the Supreme Folkie Soviet. I'm the Secretary General, so you should be fine.'

'No, I can't sing. I can never remember enough of the words. It's the Youth Theatre. Some of them want to do something.'

'Slip some acid in the stovies, no doubt.'

'They want to sing. They'll do a good job. Elaine's got a lovely voice.'

'OK, OK. I know she does, she's my niece. That's where she gets it from. The weans can sing if they want to. Lawrence'll not like it, though.'

'I don't care.'

'Dear me.'

'I may even be glad he doesn't like it.'

'Just the sort of attitude I'd expect from a bourgeois-artistic parasite. Give them a job and they won't thank you. You'd be different if you'd been through the war.'

'Graham.'

'Aye?'

'Fuck off.'

'Aye, hen, I'll probably do that. There's a tupperware box full of maggots I put to cool off in the fridge. Make them sleepy. I'll need to fetch the little buggers. We don't want Heather to find them. She'll only scream and wake them up. Ta ta.'

'Graham? Graham!'

The back of Graham's bunnet progressed serenely away.

Margaret walked outside and sat on the car-park wall, her feet on the pavement. It was cold, her breath ruffed out and vanished, reaching into the road. You never thought how far your breath might travel. You must walk through other people's breathing all the time, everyone really much closer than they thought.

It was November today. Last week had been October, now this was November and on it would go, right through, you couldn't stop a month once it was started.

Every year, in November, her father died. In March, her daddy had his birthday; June was hers; Hallowe'en and Bonfire Night and then he would die.

He did it at home without telling anyone, some time on the eleventh or the twelfth. Margaret wanted to be more exact than that, she wanted to have felt it when he died, to have noticed the time a cold came to her soul. She should have noticed.

All that his neighbours could tell her was that his lights had gone on in the evening and were never turned off. His curtains were drawn and not opened, he didn't walk out for his paper and fresh rolls. That night, in the flat below him, Mrs Mitchell didn't hear him pace.

The ambulance men found him in his reclining easy chair, the footrest up and his dressing-gown worn over shirt and trousers, dark red slippers and black socks. His hands were resting across *At Swim Two Birds* – a book he read again every two or three years. His eyes were closed.

She missed him.

'Hello?'

'Hiya, it's me.'

'Hello me. What's wrong?'

Colin could usually tell if something was wrong. Maybe he guessed from the way she made his phone ring.

'I'm fed up.'

'Is Lawrence being naughty again?'

'No, no, he's not even in. No, I just feel duff. Why are you home?'

'Decided I'd finish up early. Sold enough. I was nearly in *your* home.'

'What for?'

'I was going to raid your laundry – take home some underwear.'

'How about coming out here. If you want to.'

'What is wrong.'

'It's a bad time of year.'

'Fuck. I'm sorry, love, I forgot. I'll see you in a bit. I've got the van. OK?'

'Yeah, yeah. Thanks.'

'OK. Ta ta.'

'OK. Colin?'

'Yes?'

'I . . . thanks. See you.'

He arrived with two lemon doughnuts in separate paper bags,

two coffees in polystyrene cups and a pizza with mushrooms and ham.

'Keep your strength up.'

They drove out in the van, then stopped to eat lunch within sight of the long, grey river that filled up the empty docks. The van was parked across brown, metal tracks that slid underneath chained gates, then disappeared.

'He died tomorrow.'

'I know, I remember now. I should have thought before.'

'It's alright. I'm glad you're here.'

Colin brought out tissues and they wiped their hands before they held each other. Colin's mouth tasted of lemon and sugar. The heater and their breath steamed the windows up.

'Do you want to go home?' He spoke very quietly and after a long time.

'No, I have to go back. I'll be fine now.'

'I'll stay until closing time.'

'You don't have to.'

'I know that.'

Margaret left him in the Centre café, watching TV, somebody's toddler amusing itself with his feet.

His tea drunk, and reading the paper, Colin overheard a conversation.

'I understand your problem, hen. Dear Lord, we've all been there, but there is a solution and this is it. All we need is enough people to put their names down and we can start a credit union. Think about it — one pound isn't much, but if you've got a hundred people, all chipping in their quid . . . What have you got?'

'A hundred pounds. But I couldn't ever afford to borrow. I couldn't pay it back.'

'Not with a bank, you couldn't, but with this, the union helps you save your money, keeps it out the way of your man, you know. You get a wee bit of interest and if you want to borrow, it's only a wee bit of interest you pay. It's not like a bank – it's run by folk like me and you. They understand about bills and the wean's birthday, the way the wee ones go through clothes. They understand.'

Colin sold people satellite television; he knew when he heard another salesman sell.

'Excuse me.'

Colin stood up and turned around to see a woman at one of the tables, with a jerking pushchair parked close by. A thin-lipped man in a dark blue suit was sitting tight beside her. While he spoke, he bobbed his head like a walking pigeon, or a pecking hen.

'Excuse me.'

'Yes.' BOB.

'I couldn't help but overhear. You were talking about a credit union.'

BOB, BOB. 'I was friend, to this lady. If you would like more information,' BOB, 'I'd be glad to take your name and address when we've finished here.' BOB.

'No, that's alright. I just thought you must know a friend of mine – Bobby Sinclair – he told me all about this, last time we met.'

'Aye,' BOB, 'aye, Bobby.' BOB. 'Good man, he is.'

'Still mad for the Munro bagging, is he, up those hills?'

'Oh yes, yes, indeed.' BOB.

'Still racing whores and fucking pigeons? Come on, you can tell me, you're his pal.'

'He's doing fine.' BOB. 'I'll say you were asking for him.'

'Please do. You know, he was telling me that loan sharks put out agents where they hear a credit union's trying to start. These agents pretend they're from the union, they find out who needs money round the place, then they make them offers they can't refuse. The loan sharks don't like credit unions. I don't think I caught your name.'

'No,' BOB, 'no. I don't think you did.' BOB, TURN, BOB. 'Mrs Muir, I'm afraid that I've run,' BOB, 'out of time, just now, but I'll be back in touch, I've got your address.' BOB, BOB.

He picked up his case to leave as Colin cleared his throat and began.

'Ladies and gentlemen, could I have your attention, please? That little bastard leaving the building, just now, works for a loan shark. I don't know which one and I don't care. He may have told you he works for a credit union. That was a fib. If he worked for a credit union, he would know Bobby Sinclair, who gets about by wheelchair because he has MS. He doesn't climb too many hills, our Bobby.

'I think, before he goes, this man had better leave his address book with us, just to save things getting nasty outside . . . Thank you. I don't think you ought to come back here now, we'll remember your face.'

The man bobbed out into the doorway, silence thick behind him now. For a moment he turned and looked at Colin.

'Now I know your face, cunt. I know you, too.'

A few men made to follow him, one reaching his car with a brick, as he pulled away. Colin stayed inside with the pushchair and Mrs Muir. He bought her a mug of sweet tea, but her hands were shaking too much for her to hold it.

In his future, Colin has this memory. Mr Webster leans in close above him and speaks.

'To prove I have nothing against you as a person, I will tell you something nice: you have good teeth.'

Sometimes Colin almost dreams this now, but it always stays a little out of sight. Although he wakes with the taste of another man's breath in his mouth, he doesn't understand this and so is not afraid.

Colin dreamed tonight, this time something sunny, the air in his room turning hot and sandy.

In another bed, four miles away, hardly any distance for Colin when he jogs, Margaret is stirring. She turns on her side and shuts her eyes, holding in the sleep, the nice pictures.

This is summer. A big, honey light is falling from the kitchen window and on to the wooden table that Margaret remembers standing at the centre of the room. She watches herself, her mind in a little girl's body, sitting on the edge of the table, legs hanging down, the feet heavy. Her skin is that light, child brown it never turns now and both her knees are bloody.

There was a jump she took. Running by a wall and then jumping, a fall on to her knees. That hurt.

One knee is in the sunshine and one is not which makes the warm one feel nicer than the other. They both sting enough to make her cry from time to time.

And quickly Margaret feels happy, because she can hear her father humming. Looking down at the top of her own head and also out through three-year-old eyes, she hears his sounds. He is snipping and clattering somewhere and humming the way he does when he is busy.

Then he comes, living and moving with thick, dark hair and the sleeves of his blue shirt rolled up high on muscular, pink arms. He looks at her, leaning down and forward, so that she sees mainly the top edge of his eyes.

'Now. I'll put all this next to you. The plasters and things. No, don't look. No need to look.'

He breathes in a little, makes his eyes smile.

'Are you brave, then? I'm not brave. I hate the sight of blood.'

Margaret hears a laugh then, coming towards the table, is a woman she knows must be her mother, although she has never seemed to know what her mother looked like. The laugh is one that Margaret uses now and comes from a slightly familiar mouth. Eyebrows lift and seem very like her own. Margaret realises how little she has ever resembled her father. She only has his habits, not his looks, which seems ungrateful somehow.

Margaret's mother speaks.

'I'm not doing it, Ted. That's your job. You do that, not me.'

She laughs again, fades back and away, while little Margaret turns to her father and his bottle of iodine, his small smile.

'Well, that's decided, then. We won't like this. This will hurt. But only a bit, only for a minute and it will make things get all well. You'll be better after. You hold tight. Maybe you . . . hold on.'

He puts the bottle down and just holds a little dab of cloth, stained with iodine. His free hand reaches out.

'You hold my hand. Mm hm? If you hold my hand I won't be scared.'

Margaret sees her father's head bend over hers and kiss her hair and feels something spread, a thing she sees like fire around her legs.

The beginnings of a predicted gale is bumping up the street, singing along the telephone wires, just pleasantly melancholy and our time is 01:23. Beyond Margaret's window, parked cars are blinking as fine rain flattens on their windscreens, beads and runs. There is a slide of tyres, not far away. Colin lies on his back in the dark and hears two women laugh and then gently swear.

Margaret wakes a little, feeling one tear fall, surely from her daddy and not from her, and make a warm place on her arm. Daddy squeezes her up against him and presses her into somewhere without pain, but with fire.

Her mind dips down into another summer's day. Last year? The year before? Near there.

Some of the Youth Theatre are belly down on the grass, listening to Talking Heads. Gus and Tam and Susan are playing with fire. They've done it before. They like it.

A good, still day like this and they drink their milk, line their stomachs and out with the torches, the spirits, the flame. Probably they need no practice and are doing this more for the fun. For whatever reason, they are practising anyway. Carefully. They were trained with care and far away from Lawrence by an odd-looking man with no hair which apparently helped the fire no end.

'It's easier like this, man. You've got to be smooth. Smooth, man. And careful.'

He stared that into Gus's smile one chilly, pale morning.

'Fuck with this, it'll fuck you right back. It won't care. And you are going to have to concentrate on that more than anyone here. Your kind of attitude kills. But don't worry, it normally only kills you.'

They were all good at concentrating now. And good at fire. When Lawrence was out for the day, they would let it out of its bottle to fly away. This sometimes worried Margaret.

'One day, girls and boys, he will come back and classify you all as offensive weapons. And I will lose my job.'

'Och, lighten up, Maggie. It's too hot.'

Gus sucked a long pull from the bottle and let it out in an acrid roar of smoky orange. And again.

'Come on, finish up; it's nearly closing time.'

'So close up. We're outside.'

Susan's voice appeared by Margaret's ear.

'Why don't you try it. It's dead easy.'

'Fuck, aye. Gonny try it, eh?'

'Aye, go on.'

The sun seemed to fall sharper, to glare the gravel flat.

'No.'

'S'easy. You just spit.'

'No.'

'Have a practice. If you can do it with water. You can do it with anything.'

'Like fire.'

'Aye.'

'No. Do I look crazy?'

'Would you do it, if we said you did?'

'What do you think?'

'Yeees! Brilliant, Maggie.'

'No! That was a no. That was no.'

'She looks dead crazy to me. What do you say, Tam?'

'Crazy Maggie. Crazy as fuck.'

There was something about that. Being called 'Crazy Maggie'. Little bastards, they knew that would work. Being Crazy Maggie.

'You shower of bastards.'

'That's us. Come on.'

It was good. At first she closed her eyes, but the fourth time, she just watched what her breath could produce. It was like her soul coming out. She'd always known her soul would be that colour.

But she hadn't been there when what she dreamed now happened. She had gone inside to wash her face and rinse out her mouth which tasted truly revolting. She had smiled at the applause when she finished, even stood to catch some of it, before going inside. Her mind stays out in the sun, watching.

Gus decided to finish off the bottle of spirits. All but a few of the folk still on the grass had left and he stood with his head tipped back, sun burning along the brown glass as he swung it to his mouth. Then Lawrence's car parked down in the street and Lawrence got out. Gus spat heavily.

'You there. You. What are you doing? Are you drinking. If you're drinking, I shall call the police and you're barr – '

'I'm not drinking. If you don't swallow, it isn't drinking.'

Lawrence was closer now. For the people who could see Gus's face, he was coming too close.

'What are you doing, then? Explain.'

When Gus didn't answer, Lawrence threw the question wider. As his head turned, he started to sweat.

'What are you doing?'

Gus spoke over his shoulder to Susan.

'Turn up the music and we'll show him what we're rehearsing, eh?'

'Oh, so this is a rehearsal. I'm expected to believe – '

'Shame it isn't "Burning Down the House". That would have made it perfect.'

'Next track, maybe. Maybe.'

'Well, let's go then. Let's go.'

Gus began to walk a slow curve, forcing Lawrence into another while the music ran on, sounding oddly unpredictable in the heat and the open air. Tam passed a fresh torch to Gus who watched it thicken away from the breeze, testing the breeze. As Gus lifted the bottle, Susan moved to touch Lawrence's arm.

'I'd get out of the way, Mr Lawrence. You don't want burned, do you?'

Margaret dreams the leap and flutter of fire reflected across windows, shivering heat over walls, putting strange colour into eyes.

She dreams Gus, arched like a bird. He lets his feet dance, just a touch, careful of sudden turns in the air, the flame. He makes it safe, but lets his face show something wild; finishing the spirits in one final, exploding breath.

Lawrence may have flinched a little when Gus lifted an arm to wipe his mouth.

'What do you think, then? Mr Lawrence? Good for the kiddies' parties, pensioners' outings. What do you think.'

Lawrence seemed to come to a decision. Nobody could have said what, but he nodded his head a few times in agreement with it before he spoke.

'I think that's an interesting skill. Not useful, but interesting. The staff are inside?'

'I think so, haven't seen them since we got here. Outside isn't their territory, is it?'

'What's your name? You don't mind my asking?'

'I don't mind, I just wonder why you'd want to know.'

'Because I'm interested. Tell them, the staff, that I passed by.'

'What for?'

'Pardon?'

'Did you pass for any reason.'

'None.'

Susan turned off the music when the car had drawn away.

'And you had to have the fucking music, too. Big, cool bugger. You're off your fucking head, you know that?'

'Mm?' Gus seemed to be thinking of something else. Kicking at the gravel and singing under his breath. ' "Three hun-dred . . . six-ty five deg-rees. Burning down – " '

'I scared him, though, didn't I?'

Susan smiled, 'Aye, you did.'

'I scared *him*. I did that. It was easy, too. I didn't think it would be that easy.'

'What would be that easy?'

And Margaret walks out under the heavy sun, feels it on her face and shoulders, gravel moving under her feet, tastes the sourness of burnt spirits and sweat there, mixed with the sweetness of tired grass.

'What would be easy?'

'To do this every day, Maggie. To do this and nothing else, every day.'

Margaret falls into an undisturbed warmth, sighs out into her bedroom as she dims the sun.

The first time Gus and the others performed the fire, let it spring into a clammy dusk, all feathers and teeth, Margaret wondered how good an example she was. Where was she taking these people?

Flares of heat were almost reaching a late Gala Day crowd when she remembered the kids working all day to end by reaching down into earth and dirt for coins. They had clowned and acted; Susan and Elaine had juggled; they had worked hard and then had to stoop down and find their payment thrown at their feet like a quiet insult.

There was something uneasy about it. People's eyes on them had an ugly weight when the end of a performance came and then round and down went the hat, the hands, the money. Today the money was for a hospital, but it still felt the same. They shouted to drown the feeling.

'In his pocket or in the tin, which do you dare. Keep that Dialysis Unit running. No one else will. Hope you never need it and pay just in case – that's the way. All notes must be folded. Keep the folk alive. Thank you, thank you, thank you.'

'For fuck all. Asking the buggers to save their own skins and they look like you've spat in their eye. Jesus fuck.'

The same feeling would sink over the Factory when the pale-faced young men and women would scuff in, hoping they could get a meal, a warm. They were people it made you cold to stand close to.

If Lawrence wasn't looking, they would get their feed – no paying – and then go. One time you looked they would be there and then they would be gone, leaving a taste of frost.

Margaret would watch the Youth Theatre and wonder where they would go to. When they would go. She was almost at a dead end herself, almost past the point where she could imagine a change for the better, any change at all. That was how she felt. Prematurely finished.

She was telling these people to keep clean, to keep straight, start their lives right, but what did starting right have to do with them? And she knew, at their age she hadn't been clean, or straight, or right. They would ask her for advice sometimes and what could she tell them? What did she know? Had she learned?

She wanted, at times, to tell them about the night down South, safe in the Heart of England, when she had spread the oil on her liquorice rolling papers, then rolled them full of English grass and menthol tobacco.

Sitting by the open window, blowing the smoke at the stars and wanting Colin back. This was the house they'd been in together and now he wasn't there. She would have to go back to her father and her father's sympathy, all the time wanting Colin back. Nothing other than that.

She smoked her lungs transparent and then black and then some hot colour until she felt she wanted to lie on the floor for a long time and let the smoke rise, herself sink.

The floorboards pressed her elbows, heels, the ridges down her spine, her skull, until she was suspended by those points. A power grew in her head, that or the echo of power, and it seemed that if she touched herself now, Colin would feel it. If she thought his name enough, it would become a word in his head. If she let her wanting become a sweat, a movement, he would know. All that energy would kick off a message into space.

Rain was coming in through her window in the morning and had wet her feet. Something about the way she moved was swollen, thick, heavy. She hoped she had dreamed the reason for her lying on the floor. If it hadn't been a dream, it would mean she was much more stupid than she wanted to be.

Not crazy. Stupid. Margaret would like the Youth Theatre to know how stupid she can be.

Margaret found it odd, how she learned things. A person she knew very well could tell her something and although it would seem to make good sense, a total stranger would turn the familiar sentence round another way and there it would be – the meaning she thought she'd grasped all along, very clear and very new. So there she was again, understanding that she hadn't understood.

Or familiar people could teach her in unfamiliar ways.

Or words she had heard at school would suddenly light in her head and she would know they had been untruths, incompletions, evasions, slivers of something bigger that she hadn't listened to. She could feel the same way about university. She wanted to go back again now, because now she'd be there for herself and not her father.

Or she would go to bed and then wake up in the morning with something she hadn't known before, there in her mind. Sometimes she knew her daddy must have planted it.

'Princess? There's my Princess. You asleep?'

He was whispering so low that Margaret could barely hear him and she could tell that he was really speaking to himself. He let a path of light into her room, walked forward and then closed it off behind him. He came over gently to let his weight tug down one side of the bed. She didn't move, didn't open her eyes, knowing that he wanted her to be there, but nothing else. That was nice in a way; not as good as talking, but nice.

'There she is. All asleep. Oh, what do we do, eh? Can't stay like this. I won't be here in the end. In the end you'll have to look after yourself. All those worries, all that heaviness. We should just stay like this, then one of us would always sleep at night and, in the end, maybe I would sleep, too. That would be good.

'Princess?'

She started slightly and knew he was looking at her, felt his eyes.

'Sssh, I'll not wake you. I'll not wake you. There. No harm done. No worries, not a one.

'Not even for me really. You know that? You see, I send them away. I imagine a railway line, the two lines of track, silver lines. I imagine a station; somewhere for the train to come to, clean down the track, into the station. You can walk up and down the platform and know exactly where that train will stop, because it has nowhere else to go.

'And when the train comes? I give it my worries on board to take away. All along the silver lines, it takes them away. I promise you. And I'll make you a train like that, I do promise. It'll run on silver, straight and safe. Nothing will stop it, Princess, it'll just roll on. Past me and away. Past me.'

This seemed so sad that Margaret gave a cough and rolled over until her stomach could feel her father's side through the blankets.

'Oh, I'm sorry, I woke you.'

'Hiya.'

'There's Margaret. Eyes full of moonlight, ears full of water, what did I do to deserve such a daughter. You go back to sleep, now, I'm sorry.'

'Tell me something.'

'What?'

'Anything. A story.'

'You've had too much story already. Come on, school tomorrow.'

'I needn't go, though.'

'Yes you do need go, though. Sleep. Aaaah, come on then. We'll let the porters come and get you, my worry. Where do you want to go?'

'Blackpool.'

'Blackpool?'

'I'm only playing. Staying here is fine in real life, but it should be Blackpool for this.'

'How do you want to go.'

'Ship.'

'Oh, now then. Is it a calm sea, or a stormy sea.'

'Just calm.'

'Not a wee bit stormy?'

'No.'

'Well, we'll have to see. See the sea, eh, see the sea? Well it wasn't bad for this time of night. You look out for the typhoons, never mind screwing your face up at other people's jokes.'

And her daddy pressed and bounced his hands into her mattress, soft and then harder and then making the bed jump so much that she squealed and then soft and softer until they both rocked to a stop.

'More.'

'More tomorrow.'

'It is tomorrow.'

'Then more the day after that.'

He had kissed her on the forehead and tucked the sheets round her in a way which was uncomfortable, but nice because of the thought behind it.

He always did such nice things for her, but still kept that place inside him that stayed beyond her reach. She couldn't stop him being lonely, or pacing his bedroom floor, waiting for something she didn't understand to appear along the line. She hadn't helped him with that, or with much else. A bit of a useless daughter, really, if she thought about it.

When James taps her shoulder, Margaret turns automatically without thinking who is there. The way he looks surprises her again, as if he should appear more normal, now that she knows how normal he is inside. His blue eyes are slightly quizzical.

'What's the matter, do you want something?'

If she had to, could she get him to the toilet? What would she do once they were there?

James folds his hands together and rests them under his head.

'You were asleep?'

He nods and points to her.

'No, I wasn't sleeping.'

He smiles and nods his head, taps one hand against his paper.

SNORING   WAKE ME UP

'What? I wasn't snoring. Was I snoring?'

James giggles and claps his hands together.

'Are you serious? I've been snoring with all these people around? Seriously, James?'

James giggled again and, very shakily, wrote.

JOKE

'Joke?'

Nods and a big, fading smile.

'Joke.'

Hands clasped in an apology.

'James, you have an odd sense of humour.'

Eyes closed, head drooping.

'I could go in the huff with you.'

James begins to turn away and Margaret reaches over to point at the paper.

JOKE

'I'm only kidding, I'm not in the huff. I'm joking. James. I'm joking, OK?'

JOKE

'Yes, I'm only joking, don't be upset.'

James turns to shake his head and point at his chest.

'Oh, you were joking again.'

Nods.

'OK, well, I'll just go in the huff again, then.'

James claps his hands to his mouth, giggling, then points.

JOKE

'Yes. And. Then I'll pick you up and throw you through the carriage window and watch you bounce as we go past.'

JOKE

'Mm hm. And you can just catch hold of the last carriage and crawl along the train and climb through the window and poison my coffee in revenge.'

JOKE   GOOD   BUT

'But what?'

CANT CLIM   CANT WALK

'No. No, I know that, but, well, jokes don't have to be real. Do they?'

James nods and looks past her head, out through the window. Margaret can't think of anything to say. When she tries to pat his hand, he is writing again.

IM SECRET

'You're secret. How do you mean?'

NOWON NOWS   NOBODY

'What don't they know?'

ME

'I know what you mean, James, I think I know what you mean.'

JOKE

'No, James I do know what you mean.'

Margaret and James settle down to play noughts and crosses, slipping the grids in the spaces between James's words.

'James, why don't you just write CHEAT once and then you can point and tell me whenever you like? And I can point to it as well.'

Around them the hills grow lower and begin to cup small towns in the hollows they make. Grey stone buildings and streets pass, gathered in the lap of brown green slopes. One is shaded under boiling cloud, but marked out with fingers of brilliant light where the sun glimmers through. It seems that God is pointing at it, for some undisclosed reason, while the train noses south, hidden from time to time by embankments.

Margaret continues to play with James, because they are both happy playing games, knowing they are both capable of deeper and greater things, but knowing they can't be bothered with them now.

Colin was good at games.

Margaret had seen him play pool and football, badminton and dominoes with the same peculiar devotion. If they happened to be in a pub on quiz night he would be powerless to leave without taking part and hearing the final result. He had a competitive mind.

Alone with him, she would know he was completely cheerful when he started to play.

'OK. Minister's Cat time.'

'What?'

'Time to play The Minister's Cat.'

He nudged his prick a little more snugly in and kissed her nose.

'Some people would think this was hardly the moment, you know?'

'Nope, I can't think what you mean. Come on. Just one game. We can do other things, as well.'

He did another thing. Just a little.

'You know you're a pervert.'

'Mm hm. You've got first go, by the way.'

'Awfffffff. The minister's bloody cat is amiable.'

'That'll do for a start. Come here.'

'I am here.'

'Not close enough.'

Margaret felt him begin to bite along the line of her ear, something she didn't always like, but which seemed pleasant now. He was tight against her stomach and tight inside, slow and smooth and tight. It was surprising, sometimes, how neat a fit he could be.

'Your turn, baby.'

'I . . . um . . . the cat's amiable, bucolic, carnivorous, domineering, what was it?'

'Not concentrating.'

They were in a rhythm now, both moving, which was quite unusual. Their first real sweat began to break.

'Amiable, bucolic, carnivorous, domineering, emetic, fucking gigantic, hairy, intelligent, jocose, killer, lecherous. Now. It's the wee baby's turn, my wee baby.'

Margaret watched him, knowing that he couldn't watch her back, because both his eyes were closed and he seemed intent on reaching for something just behind her head. She felt he was reaching through her for something else she didn't know about.

'Amiablebucoliccarnivorousdomineeringenergetic, no emetic, emeticfuckinggigantichairyintelligent, intelligentjocosekiller-lecherousmalodorousniceorderlypurringquerulous. Querulous. There. Colin?'

'Thinking, just thinking of a good one, wait a minute. Oh.'

If she could reach inside him it would be different. Margaret thought that. And she wanted to make it different. There was something he wouldn't let her into. He wouldn't let it go, make it open for her to come in. She knew because she did the same thing; never entirely being there. Even though she tried.

'Purringquerulousratarsedstotioustightropewalking.'

'What?'

Colin paused a little, keeping a laugh down where they could both feel it tickle. She liked to feel him laugh and she liked to feel him at the edge of laughing almost as much.

'Tightrope walking.'

'No.'

'Why not?'

'No.'

'But why not, though?'

'You're not taking this seriously, are you? Mmm? And how are you taking this? Is this serious? Is this? What about . . . Mmm? Serious?'

'Very serious.'

'Good. Then we'll put the cat out. Put the pussy to sleep.'

'Colin?'

'What?'

'I love you.'

'I know.' He spoke very quickly. 'Really, I know, you don't even have to say it twice. I know.'

And for a while, they did serious things together.

If Margaret remembers rightly, that all happened on a Saturday night, or an early part of Sunday morning. Before they went to sleep there was already a trace of brightness over her street. She hated having to do these things on a Saturday night; the only possible times narrowing into Friday or Saturday night, because otherwise they would both be tired at their work in the morning.

She didn't like to be so limited, but there were times when it was like this – very nice and easy – and the day of the week was not important. Margaret would visit Colin's house or he would visit hers, or they would both go out together somewhere else and there would seem to be no work involved, no effort, only the pleasure of being there. She would smile past Colin's face, or down at her feet and think of her daddy's only sexual advice.

'You see, sometimes you have to work at these things. Really, you have to work at them a lot. It's not like us, it's not something you're born with; the two of you will have to choose each other and then have to make sure you were right. It's quite hard.'

'Could I not have a baby, instead?'

Margaret had been quite young when they had the conversation.

'A baby? What do you mean? Has anybody said that?'

'No, but I could have a baby and then I wouldn't need anyone else. I could be like us. You'd have a grandbaby, then.'

'Your baby would need a daddy would it not?'

'It would have you.'

'Aye, well, it's all a long way off. But, Margaret?'

'Yes?'

'Tell me if anyone says anything about babies to you. Will you do that?'

The subject didn't arise again until their positions had almost reversed. Margaret was visiting her father to check if he was eating properly, to nag him into doing less in the garden. To mother him.

'It's not just your garden, it belongs to all the flats and they pay someone to come in and work on it.'

'Margaret, all he does is cut the grass. He's just a boy. If I had to sit in all day and watch the weeds grow, I'd go daft. Do you want me daft?'

'Of course not.'

'Well.'

They would often have a proper Sunday lunch together, both eating more than was comfortable for the other's benefit.

'That was nice.'

'I'll not be moving for a while.'

'Well, I'll get on with the washing up.'

'Margaret Hamilton, since when have I been unable to do my own washing up. Sit on your backside and let your pudding settle. There's more tea, I think.'

'No, you finish it. I couldn't swallow another thing.'

'Mmm hm.'

Margaret lifted the tray from his lap and left it in his tiny, shiny kitchen. They sat for a while, hearing his clock chime a quarter hour; it didn't seem to tick, never had. Margaret breathed in the smells that always surrounded her father, even in the sheltered flat. All that was missing was a trace of coal tar soap. She'd bought him something different for Christmas and now he must be using it. Not as nice as coal tar.

She moved her eyes over the ornaments that were mostly older than her and remembered where Daddy had kept them in his old place. Their place. She moved down to sit between his legs, her back against his armchair and her arms looped up over each of his knees.

'Hullo, hen.'

'Hiya.'

'You're getting thin.'

'So are you.'

'It doesn't look well on a woman. You worry too much.'

'Uh huh.'

'You know, I think I'm into my change of life.'

'How do you mean?'

'I just don't feel the same as I did. I've asked Mrs Mitchell about it – you know, her downstairs. She just laughed. Nice lady.'

'How do you not feel the same?'

'Mainly, it's the way I think. I think about your mother a lot. Really a great deal.'

'Well, that's only natural.'

'No it's not. It's the least natural thing in the world. I haven't seen her since, what, 1963. Why on earth should I think about her now? I'll tell you something, Margaret, something I've worked out. It's important.'

'I'm listening.'

'If, when you get someone . . . Don't sigh. I'm just saying. If you end up getting close, just remember. You need to have the same sense of humour. It's the most important thing. You can get by without anything else. Your mother and I, we never laughed at anything together. All she could find to laugh at was me. That's not what you want. Get a man with the same sense of humour.'

'OK.'

'I mean it. Promise. Don't make my mistakes.'

'I promise. Honestly.'

111

He cupped his hands across her head and kissed between them. 'Good girl.'

Margaret and Colin did have the same sense of humour. Sometimes they didn't work at each other in quite the way they should, but they did, very often, laugh at the same kinds of things.

Because it is such a nice thing to see, Margaret has always wanted a picture of Colin laughing. So far, the pictures she has show him about to be laughing, or having laughed. Of course, she has an image in her head, but that won't really do. She wants better evidence than that, as if he might someday disappear and she would have to prove that he existed. With his laugh.

His laugh is important for Margaret. When Colin came back to Scotland and preferred to watch Margaret without her seeing him, he allowed himself to walk past the Fun Factory. He watched its street and grew used to the way that Margaret looked from an ever decreasing distance. This meant that when he called on Margaret, for the first time in three years, he was prepared for the meeting, but she was not.

She was sitting on her own in the Blue Room, writing a sign for the café. PATRONS ARE REQUESTED NOT TO TENDER IRISH COINS. Sam knocked the door and came in.

'There's a guy here says he knows you, Mags.'

'Knows me?'

'You're the only Margaret Hamilton we've got. Will I send him through? He looks alright.'

'Where is he now?'

'Sitting in the café. Lesley thinks she's seen him in before. This isn't something we should know about?'

'You tell me. I'll come out.'

Colin has asked her since if she knew who it would be, sitting at an empty table by the door. She can only say that she felt strange as she looked round the café and then not completely surprised when she saw his face.

'Oh.'

'Do you know him? Will I go now?'

'Sure, sure, Sammy. I know him. I think I know him.'

Colin stood almost as soon as she saw him, brushed the hair back from his forehead and took a step. Margaret turned and walked back into the Blue Room, unsure if he would understand to follow. She left open the door.

Perhaps a minute passed before she heard him walk in.

'Hi.'

'Hi yourself.'

'How are you?'

She could feel herself wondering if he meant this year, or last year, or maybe the year before. Or did he only mean today?

'I don't know, I was fine this morning.'

'Good. Good. I actually feel rather nervous myself.'

'Oh.'

'Aye. I'm not long up from London . . . that's where I was . . . I wanted to see you quite soon. How've you been? Did I say that?'

'Alright. You could have called.'

'I know, I know, I thought about it. I was going to and then I was going to write and then I was going to come up and then I wasn't. Sorry, sorry. I know.'

'I mean you could have called to say you were coming.'

'Fuck. Aye, yes, definitely. Um. See, I had things all lined up to go to like the Burrell and the Necropolis, Provand's Lordship and all that, but none of the guides had your number. I did try. Tourist Information. Fuck all. I looked.'

Margaret didn't know he'd meant to be funny until he was

already laughing, wheezing and gulping, holding it in to watch her face. If she had decided not to laugh, he would have gone away again. That would probably have been the end of that.

Instead she laughed because he really wasn't funny, but he was laughing and that was funny and both of them laughing together at something unfunny was certainly funny, in fact it was so funny that it hurt. Soon, they looked as if they had been crying, which was enough to make anyone laugh. So they did.

And one or other of them reached out a hand and one or other of them took it and Margaret thought, very clearly, 'It's alright. It's alright now.'

As if someone had turned a tap somewhere, flicked a switch, it was spring. Margaret spent the whole day tasting a certain difference in the air outside the Factory, feeling a certain kindness in the rain, watching a certain easiness in faces she was used to finding taut.

Lesley and Sam, having found out for certain that Lawrence was still away on a long weekend, chased each other slowly round the office and held hands over lunch. The domino players smiled at them, fatherly, some enjoying snacks not purchased on the premises.

When Margaret got home she didn't feel tired and there was still some daylight to make the dinner by. It was close to the end of February, just over a year before she would lose her job. Colin didn't yet have a key to her flat but he had taken to turning up there without warning on a variety of pretexts.

'Hi. Did I disturb you? I just wondered if I could use your bath.'

'My bath?'

'It's the spring weather, you know? I took the afternoon off – and most of the morning – came home and I've been running all day. Right round the park and along the river and fuck knows where. Run myself stupid, I have. And you know I've only got a shower. I need a bath.'

By this time he was standing in the hall, wriggling out of a sweatshirt while he took off his shoes.

'Christ, I'm going to be sore tomorrow.'

'Well, it's your own fault. I can remember when you wouldn't walk your length.'

'I know. I remember it, too. But me and Uncle Archie sorted it out. And I've needed to look after myself sometimes. It's better to be fit. Safer. If you wanted, you could run with me sometimes.'

'I will assume that was a joke. Should I wash some of this?'

'No, I'll have to go home in it. I suppose I'll have to go home.'

'I can lend you a big kind of sweater and I think I've got one of your shirts.'

'A big kind of sweater.'

'For your big kind of body. Get in the bathroom, if you're having a bath; you'll frighten the horses like that.'

'Come and scrub my back.'

'I've got a report to write up tonight.'

'Oh.'

'It's nearly finished, I did most of it today. If Sam and Lesley hadn't been playing Mr and Mrs Rabbit all afternoon, I'd have got it done.'

'Not doing what rabbits normally do, I hope?'

'Just mooning about and giggling, calling each other wee, daft names.'

'Sounds alright.'

'Aye, well, it was. I kept breaking off to watch them, as it happens.'

'It's nice to see people in love.'

'Colin.'

'What, what have I said?'

'Come here.'

She pushed him into the bathroom then squeezed in after him. Their reflections were waiting in the mirror above the sink. Hers kissed his.

'There. That's people in love. Now, I'm going to finish this. Put that away. I'm going to finish this and by the time you've had your bath, I'll be all yours.'

'I'd like that.'

'And I would, too.'

Colin lay for a while on the sofa, his head still warm and a little damp, rested deep in her lap. Margaret wondered why they hadn't done this before, it felt so nice. He slept until the news came on television and the music woke him up.

'Ow.'

He was wearing her dressing-gown, very short on him, and as he turned, it flared away from his legs.

'What's the matter.'

'Oh, I'd forgotten I was here. Hello. I think I'm starting to seize up. My neck's sore.'

'You shouldn't run on your neck, I've told you before; use your feet.'

'But I do have to take my neck out with me. Come down here.'

'Can't.'

'Why not?'

'You're in the way.'

They would have made love on the sofa, but an odd thing happened and made them stop.

Colin was resting his weight on her chest, almost stopping her breath when there was a pain. The further he went the more pain came and then the pain became a thing in itself, very big. Margaret felt herself scream.

'What is it? Baby, what's the matter? What? What? OK, alright. Tell me when you can, it's alright, alright. Baby, baby girl, it's alright. It's alright.'

She lay with his arms around her, panting and feeling sick. Part of her wanted him to go away. She felt Colin move a little then draw in his breath.

'Darling, there's blood on me. Did I hurt you. I'm sorry. I'm sorry. Darling. Darling, we should do something about this. What is it?'

After a while longer of being quiet, Colin slid away from her and fetched a warm flannel, a towel. Margaret moved a little, began to sit up.

'I'll do it, lie back.'

And Colin cleaned her, very gently, not letting her see the blood and kissing her stomach as he dabbed her with the towel. He asked her to let him look and she opened her legs just a little, felt his breath on her thighs and a thin stab of new pain. Over his face, she could see a shine of sweat.

'Ssh. Don't be sore, please don't be sore. You're split, you've got a little split in your cunt. Lie still. You'll be fine, you'll be fine. Please.'

She could hear his voice, as if he might cry, feel his breath very hot. She didn't know how she felt; more than anything it seemed strange that her pain could affect him so much when she was getting used to it now.

Colin sat on the floor beside her, holding her head, until she had started to doze.

'Darling, darling, you shouldn't go to sleep here, you'll get cold. Come on, slowly, very slowly, we'll get you to bed.'

And Margaret became an invalid for him, went weak in his arms, found herself agreeing she would take a day off work and go to see the doctor in the morning. Colin disappeared to wash off her blood and then returned to slip in beside her. He didn't touch her, lay very still.

When she woke in the night and turned, the pain was there ahead of her again and it seemed she had something she ought to apologise for. She felt she had done something wrong. This didn't happen to other people, other men made love to other women and they didn't bleed. Would she bleed every time now? Would she always be waiting for the pain? Colin wouldn't understand that, after a while it would surely be in his way.

He kissed her goodbye in the morning and she pretended to still be asleep. She didn't know what to say to him.

Margaret was surprised when she got an appointment. Often you couldn't be given a time the same week, let alone the same day. Busy surgery, they would say. House calls, it seemed, were no longer even possible. You were better off asking your chemist for something; better off making do, saving the cost of a prescription. If she'd told them it was an emergency, it would have made things easier, but then they would have asked for details. She could hardly announce that she had a split cunt. She didn't know if she could tell the doctor that. But Margaret rang and found she was lucky: they had a cancellation.

Margaret's doctor was a sandy-haired man with a butcher's complexion, raw pink. He wore bow-ties and waistcoats and seemed to sweat a lot even though, naturally, the heat never reached his hands which remained medically chilly.

'Ah, you're looking at my little graph. Well, that shows our practice averages to date. Only sensible. See here – the number of times we prescribe, ages, sexes, drugs. Of course, with the older clients things become different. There we're only preventing death, really. Putting it off a bit. You know?'

'Aren't you always doing that?'

'Ha, ha, ha. Well, yes, of course, if you want to look on the black side . . . yes. Do you look on the black side? Often?'

'I don't know. Why I'm here . . .'

'Yes. You don't mind if I have a biscuit, do you? If I don't eat at regular intervals, I get very short-tempered. Do go on; why you're here?'

'Well, you see, last night, we had some difficulty – '

'Say no more. Time to slip up on the couch. Take off your things and give me a call when you're ready. I'll just wash my hands; crumbs, you know.'

Margaret didn't like to show herself to somebody like this. She tended to feel she was private property, something she might decide to share, but otherwise not an object to be stared at. Medical places always made her feel she didn't belong entirely to herself, because they knew better than she did what she was, how she worked. It felt strange. She supposed you could get used to it, if you had to.

Above the couch there was a clear, large notice in black and white, listing all the charges for a range of services: vaccination certificates, variously exhaustive medicals, screenings and tests.

The final sentence read, 'Removal of pacemaker from body after death: £31.30'.

Margaret read and looked away. She wondered where they would do such a thing. Why? Was it possible to use a pacemaker again? Were they cheaper, second-hand? How much did it cost to remove one before death? Could you be insured against that happening by mistake? The notice didn't mention that.

'That's quite a deep fissure you have there and one . . . inside. Did that hurt? One, nasty one inside. This is lack of lubrication, you know? Could be your pill, could be your cycle is changing, could be almost anything. How do you feel?'

'Sore.'

'Ha. Yes, but how do you feel? You find your partner attractive? Mm hm. Not depressed?'

'No, he's fine.'

'I mean, you're not depressed.'

'Well, I'm not exactly happy, right now.'

'Quite. Clothes on '

The doctor gave Margaret two prescriptions, one for anti-depressants and one more for iodine cream.

Walking away from the surgery, Margaret found the sky too blue to look at. Down the pavements there were sparrows chasing pigeons chasing crumbs. The examination had made things much more painful when she moved and she wanted to be home and lying down.

She was in just that position when Colin rang her. She had recently applied a layer of sticky, stinging, yellow cream but had not taken an antidepressant. Margaret had thrown that prescription away. She would rather be happy independently, or even not happy at all; at least she would know where she was. There were women in the Factory on Ativan, Librium, Valium, Tamazepan and the rest, nobody knew where they were. They would forget they were eating in the middle of a meal, they would stare between walls that nobody else could see, they would cry. Margaret didn't want to be like that.

Colin wanted to know if she felt depressed.

'I'm fine. I've got cream. It's nothing fatal. The split isn't, anyway – the cream's a bugger.'

'Poor baby. Will I come round?'

'It's alright.'

'I got you some chocolates.'

'It's really alright. I'm better off on my own.'

'I want to know how you are.'

'How I am is fine, but I don't need company. Not you.'

'Thanks a lot.'

'I don't mean it like that.'

'I think the meaning's pretty clear.'

'And I think you've misunderstood me. I feel funny. I don't know how I feel. I don't know when we could make love again.'

'Oddly enough, that wasn't all I was thinking of. Jesus Christ, I'm worried about you. Did the doctor say it was my fault? Is there something I can do?'

'It's my fault – I am insufficiently lubricated for you. Like an old car. I'm sorry. I want to be here for you.'

'For fuck's sake, do you think I can't do without my hole for a week or two?'

'No.'

'Well, what the hell *do* you think. Except that you don't want me round there.'

This wasn't the conversation that Margaret had wanted to have; she could feel her stomach shrinking into a cool weight, feel herself running out of words. His voice had changed. He sounded angry, but not quite.

'I'm sorry. I don't feel well.'

'Of course you fucking don't. Nor do I. What did the doctor give you? Are you taking it?'

'Cream. I said. It stings a lot.'

'Well, don't feel you have to do anything about that like getting it changed, or taking some paracetamol, just you suffer on your bloody own. OK? I'll call you sometime.'

And when Margaret said his name, his receiver was down. She sat for a while without moving, wondering who should ring whom back. Over time, she had developed a superstition that an argument was only serious if it left her with a pounding feeling in her chest. That was the sign that permanent harm had been done, because it was the way she always felt when something very bad happened. Just now, she felt fine: odd and sore and slightly angry, but not bad.

She tried to make herself dinner, but couldn't think of something she wanted to eat. She turned on the television and flicked through a variety of news. She walked into the hall and put on her coat. The idea of visiting Colin took her mind off the split. And if he wasn't in, the walk would do her good. Just take it gently, small steps.

The Underground was nearly empty. Her carriage roared and screamed its way down electric tunnels with no obvious signs of alarm. Margaret watched the blurs of brickwork and the clear, blue sparks, feeling silly because this always made her nervous. The loop ran beneath the river and she would think, sometimes, of water pressing and pounding in, or of trains colliding somewhere quite near and then lying in wait. Then crash upon crash upon crash. Because she understood how her mind could work, she ambushed herself with the thought that disasters always came when you least expected, so she must really be safe.

She rose on the escalator, unscathed, and wondered if Colin would be there, what he would say.

'God, I don't feel frightened about this. I feel alright. Is this alright? I want this to be alright. Don't make him upset. Don't make him out.'

Even walking along his close, she could smell him, his mixture of smells. His door was just at the foot of the stairs, a light showing honey through the glass. She rang the bell and watched his shadow in the hall.

'Hello.'

'This is a surprise.'

'I was passing.'

'I thought you didn't want to see me.'

'Don't be like that. Can't I come in?'

'Now you're here. Aye. Why not.'

They paused beside each other as they walked to the sitting-room. About now, in the doorway, they would normally have kissed. Colin turned and brushed his hand by her cheek.

'Hello.'

She paused to look at him.

'Hello.'

'You make me very angry, you know that? You never believe I care. I went away and left you once: alright, I know that. But you never forget it, you won't let it go, so where does that leave me? Mm?'

'I do know you care. But I feel. I feel funny just now.'

Colin noticed she was crying before she did. He ran his finger just beneath her eye and there were suddenly tears, a weakness rising from her chest and into her throat. They walked to sit on the sofa and Colin licked her eyes slowly while she tightened her arms around his waist.

'James? Tell me something.'

His face works its way round until it is pointing at Margaret in the way he would like.

'What do you think of doctors? Do you go to doctors?'

ARSOLE

Margaret laughs too loudly for heads in the carriage not to snap round, see James and snap back again.

'Funny you should say that. We must have the same doctor.'

NO DIFFREN

'Yeah, I suppose so.'

WAN ME BE DIFFREN SHAPE I SAY NO

'I don't understand, James.'

DIFFREN

'There's a "t" at the end of that.'

DIFFRENT FUC

'OK, take it easy.'

MEAN THEY NOT LIK ME AS I AM

'I'm sure they do like you. I'm sure they do.'

NO

'I like you as you are.'

CHEAT

'I'm not playing. No games.'

JOKE

'No, serious. Very serious.'

James held her eyes.

'Anyway, about doctors. You and my father, his name was Ted. Ted. Nice name. He . . . well you and I and he, we all agree about doctors. He never went near one if he could help it. He said it wasn't a coincidence that hospitals were full of people who had seen their doctor recently. And you could never talk him round, he was very decided.'

It had been raining when her daddy came back from hospital; some thunder earlier when Margaret opened his flat to put things in his fridge, turn on the heating, boil the kettle perhaps twenty times, look out of the window.

He stepped down from the ambulance in a jacket and shirt, no tie; as if he'd just got out of jail. The weight of the rain seemed to make him stoop. When she opened the door and saw him, she could think of nothing to say. Loose threads of hair had fallen down over one eye and his clothes seemed too big for him.

'Hello, Princess.'

One arm swung up, almost out of control, and flattened a hand on her shoulder. She kissed his forehead, smoothed back his hair.

'Oh.' He tried out a smile.

'Hiya, come in. You're soaking.'

'Not really. Just tired. Lord, I'm tired.'

'The kettle's just boiled.'

'Of course. Wouldn't be home without tea.'

He stopped moving into the sitting-room, just came to a halt while Margaret walked on. He swayed when he took in a breath.

'Margaret?' He'd never said it like that before. Never exactly that way. 'Margaret?'

'What?'

'Would you give me a hug?'

'Wh – Of course.'

'Thank you.'

She isn't sure why she only knew it then, but feeling his face so tight in her hair made her realise that he was taking in her smell. He was inhaling what she was and keeping that safe. Maybe she noticed it that time, because he felt a little desperate, final.

'There's my Princess.'

'Mm hm.'

She tried not to look up at his face because her worry would worry him. And she might cry.

'What are we waiting for, then? If the kettle's boiled, tea would be nice.'

'It's your house, you don't have to ask.'

'I know that. But you've made it nice to come home to.'

'Well . . .'

'Mm hm. Oh, that's a better chair than they have there. They want you lying down all the time so they put out chairs you can't sit on. God. God, God, God.'

Margaret felt very far away when she had reached the kitchen.

'Are you alright?'

'I am now. I'm not going back there.'

'What?'

'Don't look like that. I'm not going back, that's all. No panic.'

'But if you have to.'

'I'm not going back.'

'Dad.'

His shirt was damp. The rain. He should have taken it off.

'Don't worry. Look, they know I have something wrong with my heart and there's nothing much they can do, but they would love to try feeling about, in any case. I can't let them do that. It would kill me. Really. I won't die. I mean, I won't die because I don't go back there. In the end, I will. I will go away.'

'Sssh.'

'Sorry, I'm tired and I'm miserable. Sorry.'

'It's alright.'

'No, it's not alright. These places aren't meant for people and I'm a person and I will stay that way.'

'OK.'

'Thank you.'

When their tea was poured and they were both sitting, he coughed and let a sentence slip into the quiet between them.

'I did my best.'

'I know.'

'I did the best I could. I didn't know any better. Mm? I'd do it differently now.'

'You've no need to.'

'I'd be different with you.'

'Don't.'

'I would.'

'Sssh. I love you. I love you.'

This time she pressed her face into his hair. He held her away very slowly.

'Your tea will go cold. Go on. Drink it up. You should dress like a woman sometimes, you know?'

'Uh huh.'

'Uh huh. Go on and sit down.'

James nudges her with his forearm.

?

'Mm? Oh, I was just thinking about doctors, that kind of thing.'

BOR

'What?'

YOU BORIN

'Well, you'd better talk to me then, or I'll go back to thinking and be even more boring. Cheeky bastard.'

OOOO SHOCKED

For the second time, Margaret laughed too loudly to go unnoticed and James joined her, applauding softly.

Margaret didn't have to visit her doctor again. She healed quite quickly and her pain went away. Her fear of the pain also faded, with a little more time. Another year will pass before Colin has his pain, a pain which will surprise them both.

He will wake in the chill, misty morning left by a clear, clear night with Mr Webster kneeling on his arms. Webster's face cranes over him, upside down. Colin will find himself unable to speak, but will listen to Mr Webster speaking with such a focus of attention that he will later remember everything, even the spaces where Mr Webster takes his breath.

'Good morning. I like you. If I didn't, you'd be waking up alone, something it's always extremely unpleasant to do. And especially nasty in your position. No, don't move, relax, just lie, just listen. Don't move.

'Let me tell you why you're here. Why this happened. What I believe. Colin, my good friend, I believe we must learn from everything. I believe that nothing ever happens by accident.

'While you're here, you can be learning. You must. Smell the air. I've opened the windows for you, smell the air. It tells you about the city, Colin, everything. Smell the bricks and the sandstone, beginning to warm; smell the edge of traffic, the coming of heat. Smell last night's piss and the pigeons and the drunk man propped in the street beside his hat. I can smell him dying while the city wakes. It's all there for me, clear; I can breathe that in. There is nothing deeper in me than my lungs and I can breathe all of that in. Right in.'

Colin watches Webster's upside down mouth, the teeth clamping and opening, clamping and opening. Quite full lips.

'Let me tell you a secret. It's the biggest, easiest secret in the world. The clearest of clear things, so simple it makes me laugh. Right out loud, I'll laugh. At any time.

'What is it? I'll tell you. We're going to die. You and me, Colin, we're going to die.

'Sssssssh. Not now. Even *you* won't die now. Sssssssh, my wee man. But we will all die. Everybody forgets that, you know? Listen.'

Colin feels cool, smooth hands slid beneath his ears and cupping his neck. There is a tension in Webster's voice, a hardness which appears as something soft, deep, hot.

'You mustn't forget. Not ever forget. You have to burn your light through, Colin, drink it all down, have it all inside you. Do every tiny thing you want to do. It's the small things that matter, you'll always regret the small things you left undone; the time you didn't touch her face; the days you went walking in springtime and didn't fucking look at where you were; the sun. Have you ever thought about the sun? The set, the rise, the curve of the sun? You don't get a day again, Colin, it's gone and you have to take another one, there's no time to go back. Fill that time, feel it, you must. If you don't, then what we've done here can make no sense. We might have to do it all again: waste everyone's time. Be alive, Colin, don't forget.'

Mr Webster puts his thumbs on Colin's eyelids and pulls them back.

'Look at me, Colin and don't forget. You have to find out how to live.'

Then the thumbs are lifted off and Colin feels a kiss come on his forehead, then a flutter of breath before the weight leaves his forearms. An incomprehensible pain he has, surges again and hard shoes start to walk away from him. In the air there is a trace of aftershave. Mr Webster's voice appears again, far away to the left, echoing off empty floorboards and bare walls.

'When I leave, I will call an ambulance and then they will call the police. Feel free to tell them anything you like. After all, it's a free country. We need only exercise our common sense. Mmm?'

There was a smile in Webster's voice. Colin could feel it even as it drew up and back, quite out of sight.

'This was a good lesson, Colin, don't forget it. Don't forget.'

The ceilidh was set now, it had a date. Graham announced it officially one early October afternoon. He stood on the café counter, tapping lightly at a mug with one of Heather's serving spoons.

'Your undivided attention please. Ladies and domino players, I have the unalloyed joy of announcing that the Grand Unstoppable Fisherman's Ceilidh will take place on Friday the Eighth of December, from half-past eight until early the following morning, at which point a full English breakfast will be served on the croquet lawn I would encourage you to tell your friends and relations the good news, dispatch urgent telegrams to economic refugees in distant parts and generally beat the drum. The evening will only be adjudged successful if scores of you die happy in a wild conflagration of song. I thank you.'

Graham's oration ended with a moment which many would find at least confusing, if not magical.

Mr Lawrence's door snapped open and revealed Mr Lawrence's form. Every eye ticked round to meet him. Graham's form snapped first upward and then down behind the counter, seeming at one point to almost float, and then descend a little faster than his hat. Mr Lawrence's gaze raked round to the counter, pulling with it the attention of the whole, still room. Perhaps sixty eyes, in various pairs, stared at the space where Graham must surely be and found nothing, or less than a flicker of a falling hat, a passing distortion of normal sight. Lawrence almost staggered, pulled back by the hand he had left tight round the doorknob. He cleared his throat and then almost whispered, 'Keep the noise down,' before disappearing back into his office again.

Slowly, from table to table, people began to applaud, in perfect silence, always keeping a little air between their hands, so the palms wouldn't meet. There was laughter, utterly smothered, and great, shouting absences of sound. Normality only began to return when Graham had emerged from the gentlemen's toilet and taken his bow.

In the time it took for Graham to buy his tea and pick a seat, choices were made. Everyone knew that Graham had jumped behind the counter, not vanished at will, everyone knew he had slipped along against the wall and darted into the toilet from the kitchen door. He had not transported himself. But everyone chose to believe in magic, in transportation and vanishing.

Margaret missed the whole thing. She was in the office, taking a call.

'Hey, Graham.'

'Hey, Maggie! Hiya Crazy. Got the date in your diary? Eighth December.'

'Um? Oh. Yes. Yes. But what's all this I've heard about you. Your disappearing act.'

'Och, that wasn't anything. Just other folk's daftness. Ignore them, hen.'

'No really, it sounded very impressive. I wish I could disappear whenever Lawrence was after me.'

'You can.'

'Show me.'

'Hand in your notice, quit. Nothing can happen now that'll change him, this place is just going to die. We'll move on when we have to. Just leave.'

'I can't.'

'We won't thank you for it.'

'I don't expect you to; you're not why I'm staying. I couldn't get a job anywhere else. This is all I'm qualified to do.'

'Do this somewhere else.'

'It would be the same.'

'Can't help you, then. You can only disappear if you want to; if you know how. Or other folk can help you. Polismen, they're very good at disappearing folk. Tell you the truth, hen, I'm pissed off with all this magic shite. It seems to have caught the boys' imagination. Know what they call me now? Magician Graham. Well, if I was a fucking magician I'd really be disappeared. I'd be out of the close with the whoor above me and the junky underneath; I'd have no poll tax overdue. I'd be out there writing my novels, singing my songs, *choosing* not to shop in Marks & Spencer's because their food is overpriced and shitey and the entire fucking place is completely obscene. Flying the flag across Europe with their Melton Mowbray pork pies when how many folk in this city, just in this city, needn't bother their arses with going in. No point. What would we buy? What would be in our price range? Magician Graham? Magician nothing. Not to mention my private life.'

'I'm sorry.'

'Of course you are. What human being wouldn't be. Doing something about it, now that would be magic.'

'Graham . . .'

'It's alright, I'm just brassed off. It isn't you. It isn't you.'

'Has something happened?'

'No, well no really. Nothing out of the ordinary. Sometimes it feels worse than usual, I suppose. Nothing's happened.'

'Well, if you need to talk or anything, if you want a sit in the quiet. You know.'

'I won't hesitate to ask. But if I want to sit in the quiet, I just go home. There's no one else there, now. If you get my meaning. Old, tired and single again. You're a good girl, get out of here, will you.'

'Thanks a lot.'

'You know what I mean. I wasn't born at the right time. Maybe you were.'

Margaret found herself holding his arm, pulling into a hug. They patted each other's backs, slightly embarrassed already, and then parted.

'Anyway. That's enough of that. Magician Graham and Crazy Maggie, eh? They must have been thinking of somebody else.'

'You never know.'

'Aye, well, I've got flies to tie. As they say in piscatorial circles. Ta ta.'

Margaret walked away, now thinking of Colin when she hadn't been before.

Colin wasn't thinking of Margaret, because his mind was occupied with other things. Today he was having his second session with the fat, giggling acupuncturist. As Margaret looked down the list of CVs waiting to be typed, Colin lay in his underpants and shirt on the articulated couch, thinking how warm and relaxing the little room was – that he might go to sleep.

'You're getting sleepy?'

'Aye, a wee bit.'

'Well, this isn't hypnotism so . . .'

'Ow.'

'You need to keep a little alert sometimes, so that I know how things are feeling.'

'That was sore, actually.'

'You want it to be less sore, go to a European acupuncturist. I happen to think this doesn't work so well, if it is less painful.'

'Was that a racist remark?'

'No, that was a personal remark. If you think I am a Chinese racist, why let me put needles into you. If I was capable of such feelings, surely I would be capable of anything.'

'I was only kidding.'

'Uh huh.' And he began to sing, smooth, Sinatra style, 'Into each life, some rain must fall, but too much . . .'

'This the cabaret?'

'No. This is for my personal enjoyment and the delight of any individual with a degree of musical appreciation. But now we should both concentrate. I am about to adjust the needles. So, first here, stomach.'

Mr Ho padded around the elevating surface, tapping skin and twisting needles, placing them more deeply. He hummed and smiled, hands cool and curiously smooth. The stiffness and pain which had been in Colin's ankle disappeared and Mr Ho altered the balance of earth, fire, water, air and wood, because he was a thorough man and liked people to be healthy, not only free from pain.

'Why did you come here? Why not just take a painkiller? There are many available.'

'I don't take drugs.'

'Sometimes one has to.'

'Tell me about it.'

'This is a problem?'

'Not any more. I prefer not to take anything, in case I get too fond of it. That's all.'

'You become fond of these things.'

'Can do. Like I say, it's not a problem.'

'This is not a situation unfamiliar to the East. Your country kindly provided us with opium, like the CIA today. Such things are ideal for capitalism: they build their own market. Inevitably.'

'That wasn't my country, that was England.'

'I beg your pardon. When colonialists are abroad, they all look the same.' He giggled, somehow boyishly, although he must have been in his fifties. Perhaps older. 'I will simply mention that I cannot give you any acupuncture which would be effective for a fondness you might have. I cannot put needles in your soul.'

'Did I ask you to?'

'In case you might. I like to make improvements but sometimes this is impossible and it depresses me. I don't like to be depressed. What you will feel now is the rushing of energy, flowing around your body. I am opening gates to correct and assist the flow. Remember to be careful when you leave, you may be unsteady on your feet. Really, don't smile. Wait until you have to stand.'

'Mr Ho?'

'Yes, Mr McCoag?'

'You know about acupuncture.'

'You should hope so.'

'So there are all these points connected to all of these other points and you can apply pressure in one place and make an effect in another.'

'I know what you are going to ask.'

'How.'

'I can see it in your eyes.'

'My eyes are shut.'

'Still. You want me to tell you?'

'Aye, wire in.'

'Well, you have considered the nature of acupuncture, perhaps read some pamphlets, seen a diagram or two, and you know that inoffensive places in the body, hands, feet, face; very commonplace and public areas . . .'

'Aye, aye . . .'

'These are attached to more private places. You want to know where you should touch her.'

'Alright. You win.'

'You wonder if, for example, you can squeeze her hand in the street some special way and have remarkable effects. Other things, not in the street . . .'

'I gather from your tone, you're not going to tell me.'

'Think about it, Mr McCoag. If I told you these little secrets, where would be the advantage in my spending years in the study of acupuncture? You find out for free?'

'For twenty quid.'

'Twenty pounds buys this very excellent treatment.'

'Aye, I forgot. Funny how you get used to the needles.'

'Well, now you will have a great deal of time to get used to them. I am going to sit at my desk in silence and you are going to lie here for twenty minutes, allowing the process to take effect. Now. Hush. Thank you.'

So Colin lay and had the warmth from the gas fire a little more on one leg than the other, noticed a tingle or a sting at a point on his foot, his leg, his hand. Something travelled along lines he only recognised from times when they had carried pain. He felt very odd.

The needles were eventually removed, neatly, but with a final, definite bite and Colin dressed. He was shaky and had to sit down before he pulled his trousers on. Mr Ho smiled.

'Did I mention you might be unsteady for a while?'

'Yes, you did and yes, I didn't believe you.'

'Uh huh. Mr McCoag, you should come back and see me in two weeks' time. Even though your ankle will give you no trouble now. I will see you then. Oh, yes. And.'

'And what?'

'If you study the books available on acupuncture, you will broaden your appreciation of your health, change a part of your perspective. And, as far as public and private places to touch people are concerned, you will be able to find out all you want to know. I am far more sympathetic than I look, hm?'

Mr Ho stood with his arms folded across his chest, glasses pushed up on his forehead, possibly to leave room for his broad, broad smile. Colin smiled back.

'I think you're a nice man, Mr Ho. Very nice.'

Colin continued to visit Mr Ho, every now and then, returning with tiny red patches on his skin where the needles sat. Margaret would sometimes kiss them and wondered how he would look with the needles in. She didn't like to imagine it.

One day, Colin brought the news that Mr Ho would like to sing at the Fisherman's Ceilidh. His name was added to the growing list, Ignatius Ho, along with the banjo and guitar players, drummers and penny whistlers, singers and a lady who played the spoons.

From the first week in November, Graham posted a catalogue of turns for the Ceilidh on the café wall.

'Look on my works, ye Lawrence, and despair. From the four corners of the world; from The Ranton and Feegie Park, lo, they come. It's gonny be a gallus night.'

In the dead time, just before closing on a Wednesday afternoon Margaret noticed a visitor standing in front of the latest edition of the list. Bobby The Dug was clicking the last of a dominoes game back into its box, Heather was quietly mopping the kitchen floor and it was almost time for everyone to go. The visitor had bent her head a little, concentrating on the list, both hands tight around a pale Factory mug. In Jaeger fawn with a broad-brimmed hat she was enough to drive out Bobby ahead of time. Standing by the doorway, Margaret heard his whispered, ''Night.'

The day's cigarette smoke was sifting down, milky blue, and the mumbling television sparked off.

'Excuse me.'

The hat twitched round when Margaret spoke, showing her a yellowed, slightly distant face.

'Excuse me.'

'Yes.'

'We're closing now.'

'I know that, thank you.' Black, little eyes flickered at Margaret and she felt as if she might have said something wrong. The conversation seemed to have been ended.

'I'm sorry, but everyone has to leave now. I need to lock up.'

'I was reading your little list here, for your little ceilidh. What an amusing night you'll have.'

'I hope so. Have you finished reading?'

'Oh, I've finished, I've finished alright. And now you're anxious to get me out on the street.' She produced a thin, hacking laugh. 'I'm very quick on the uptake, you know. I understand where I'm not wanted.'

Margaret felt she would have to conduct this conversation on tiptoe and wished that Lesley or Sammy were still there.

'It's not that you aren't wanted, we just have to shut. Everywhere has to shut sometime. I'm sorry. Is there anything you wanted to know about the ceilidh?'

Again the laugh jerked out. 'Know about it. What could I possibly not have guessed? Please. My husband has been boring

me rigid about it for weeks. He's decided I should go. I'm getting
let out for the night. Only if I promise to behave. And guess what,
little miss, guess what?'

'I don't know what.'

'I haven't promised. Do you know why?'

'I'm afraid I don't.'

'Well, of course not. I suppose you've led a sheltered life, hm?
The thing is, I wouldn't promise that little bastard I'd spit in his
face. No promises. You have a boyfriend? Yes, of course you do.
Well, promise him nothing. Take my advice. Promise all the little
bastards fuck all.'

The visitor held up her mug and let it drop, so that Margaret
had to stretch and catch it. She began to walk slowly for the door,
leaving a thick scent behind her, something stale and expensive
and somehow unclean. Margaret noticed the stranger's suit could
do with pressing and knew without anyone saying, that the
woman was Daisy Lawrence. Mr Lawrence's wife.

Margaret caught herself thinking of Daisy all that night. The
smell of her seemed to linger, like a guilt.

But the following day, it was Mr Lawrence who slipped into
the office and let a paper fall on to Margaret's desk.

'Know anything about this?'

'I'm sorry?'

'Margaret, it seems every time I see you, you apologise. What
is it you're so sorry for – bad thoughts?'

'Mr Lawrence . . .'

'That's alright, I don't expect a confession, right now. This
notice – copies were plastered all over the Centre and we can't
have this kind of thing on display – more on principle than
anything else. No permission was asked. It's a piece of nonsense
from a head filled with more of the same, but we don't want
nonsense all over our walls, now do we? This is a building to be

proud of. We need to keep it that way. I've told you why there are vandals?'

'Lack of pride.'

'Lack of pride; architectural pride. I don't mean to patronise.'

He perched with one leg slung along the edge of Margaret's desk.

'You're learning how to keep control; I know that; I watch. But you'll need to keep on your toes for this ceilidh. I'm relying on you for that. Trusting you.'

'I'll do my best.'

'Mm, of course. You know, it's sometimes difficult to talk in here. I know that. Often, I go to the restaurant in Bridge Street.'

He paused, as if he saw something in her face.

'Well, more of a café really. We could discuss things more easily there. What you thought you might do in the future, the long term, and so on.'

'Well, I'm quite busy, just now.'

'Oh, I know, I know. But when the boss tells you to take some time off . . .' He rested on the edge of a smile.

'I would probably take some. Perhaps go away for a while.' His eyes were closing over, somehow, as she watched, so she thought she might as well go all the way. 'Did I mention, I met Mrs Lawrence, I met your wife, the other day. I think. Nice lady.'

'Kind of you to say so, but I don't guarantee she'd return any compliments. She's not good at them. Where were you thinking of going?'

'Where?'

'If the boss said – '

Lesley backed through the door with two coffees and Lawrence was standing by the filing cabinet with his hands in his pockets before she could turn and face the room. He seemed to enjoy the manoeuvre, the tension of a secret to be kept.

'You will bear that in mind, then, Miss Hamilton?'

And he left, smiling a little, rubbing his cheek with the knuckles of one hand.

'Who rattled his cage?'

'I didn't know you needed to. Why is it that nobody else is ever here when he wants to talk to me?'

'For the same reason that you're never around when he gets tore into me or Sammy. Divide and rule. Although, to tell you the truth, I don't think he likes you.'

'You don't say.'

'Just an impression I get.'

'Well, now that you mention it, I would rather have him throwing knives at my head than go through another one of his cosy chats.'

Lesley snorted over her mug.

'What, Lawrence?'

'You know what I mean.'

'Him?'

'Getting friendly, you know.'

'Naw. He's had it removed. Naw. Not Lawrence. God, that's disgusting. He must be FIFTY. And those wee, buggy eyes. Oh, nooo. If he got really excited, they'd flee right out.'

'I'm really glad you find it funny. He'll have more than his fucking eyes missing, if he keeps on slabbering over me.'

'You're not as nice as you look, you know that?'

'No, I'm not.'

'Still, Colin loves you, eh?'

This was a cue for Lesley to move the conversation back on to safer ground. Since Colin had come on the scene, Margaret felt her position with Lesley had changed. Margaret could now be gossiped with, she could learn about Sammy's more intimate peculiarities, she could at any time be cross-examined on anything from wedding plans to vaginal stimulation. Margaret realised there was a bright side to having few friends. She glanced down and began to read the illegal sheets of paper Lawrence had left on her desk.

THE CEILIDH
NOTES FOR THOSE NEW TO THE COUNTRY OR
OTHERWISE UNINFORMED

The purposes of the ceilidh, a uniquely unsullied flowering of Scottish culture, are many. Among these are the taking of spiritous liquors, the singing of songs, the playing of music, dancing, joking, wynching, fighting, greeting, eating stovies and looking at the moon while vomiting or contemplating the certainty of death. These activities are both tempered and inflamed by the presence of musical instruments, weans and men and women, each of the opposite sex.

Some activities, such as eating and singing, or fighting and looking at the moon are often considered mutually exclusive. Others, such as the taking of drink and greeting, or the singing of certain songs before a fight would seem to be inseparable.

The truth of the matter is less simple. Within the ceilidh, in its twists and turns of temperaments and times, all things may coincide. A woman may drink and fight while joking, a man may vomit while eating stovies and having a good greet. And in the process of wynching anyone may do anything at all.

As ceilidhs are often mistaken for purely musical affairs some mention must be made of this part of their nature. Instrumental music for a ceilidh must inspire either greeting, or dancing, or both, and preferably have a title in The Gaelic. Songs may deal with a range of suitable topics, for example: dying at the fishing, dying at your work, or dying at the wars. You may also brush against the beauties of nature, the lot of the common man and the bitter death of heroes. The remainder of songs will deal, very often in Scots, with getting your hole, not getting your hole, getting your hole and not wanting it, wanting your hole and not getting it, liking your hole having got it, liking your hole but wanting it better, one man getting his hole with lots of women, one woman getting her hole with lots of men, sailors, true love and having babies.

As the Israelites in slavery had their psalms, so we have the ceilidh. As the Africans transported to Haiti kept their voodoo, so we have the ceilidh. As every languageless, stateless, selfless nation has one last, twisted image of its worst and best, we have the ceilidh. Here we pretend we are Highland, pretend we have mysteries in our work, pretend we have work. We forget our record of atrocities wherever we have been made masters and become comfortable servants again. Our present and our past creep in to change each other and we feel angry and sad and Scottish. Perhaps we feel free.

Margaret knew that Graham would deny ever writing a word. He was modest, that way.

'Don't move. Stand still.'

'What? What's the matter?'

Margaret was standing frozen in her own doorway, Colin there in the dark of the hall saying that she shouldn't move.

'Nothing the matter. Just don't move.'

He stared until she began to blush, then walked forward to hold her head and kiss her.

'What was that all about?'

'You looked like a film. Just like a film. There in the doorway, waiting to come in with your bag in your arms and your hair all wild. Filmstar. I'd like to take a picture of you like that.'

'You're off your head.'

'For thinking you look like a filmstar?'

'Don't get grumpy,' she pulled back a touch from their embrace, 'I mean that you are generally off your head. Nothing specific. Which is good because I like you off your head.'

The ceilidh was gathering shape and closing fast and Margaret realised she was falling in love.

She had fallen. It was something impossible to realise until it had already come. Now she could remember being less in love, differently in love, improperly in love and she could see an alteration. She had crossed a line. This would change, too, the way she felt would always change, but now she could only foresee a deepening, a growth. It seemed to be a matter of faith and made her very happy.

When they made love it was better, too.

Even the Factory seemed a little brighter, despite the weather. Folk would appear in the doorway, faces raw with the wind, needing help with their benefits, hemmed in by forms, and they would ask about the ceilidh. They would offer to cook or to help behind the bar, to sing. A woman arrived and offered her dead husband's pipes for anyone able to play them. Just to see them in use again. Lawrence kept mainly to his office and often left early.

The Youth Theatre were on a constant and entirely natural high. Elaine had polished 'Fareweel Tae Tarwathie' until you could see the whaler's sails when you closed your eyes, tall in fields of ice. She made you feel the cold. Gus and Tammy had something unmentionable planned which they would only rehearse in secret and, in the midst of solos and harmonies and rasping throats somebody's cousin turned up. She was called Toaty Boady and may have been three feet tall but was probably less. Nobody knew how old she was, somewhere either side of seven was the guess. Margaret first saw her sitting on Gus's knee and singing 'Teddy O'Neil' like a tiny, lonely angel. Gus was crying.

'She makes everyone do that, it's something she's got. Fucking loud for a wee yin, too, eh?' He smiled and blew his nose.

Toaty Boady didn't like strong language. 'You fucking swear in front of me and I'll tell your auld man. I'm only a wean.'

So Margaret went through her days quite painlessly and spent slightly more time than usual with Colin. They now had copies of each other's keys.

'Jesus Christ!'

Margaret woke from her doze on the sofa. Colin was kneeling beside her.

'What?'

'Fuck, it's you. Don't creep up on me like that.'

'I didn't creep. You were sleeping. I could have tap-danced and you wouldn't have heard.'

'You could have been anyone.'

'Hardly. Who else has a key?'

'You know what I mean.'

'You're grumpy when you first wake up, you know that? I'll make some coffee.'

Margaret rubbed the stiffness from the elbow she had lain on and then followed Colin into the kitchen.

'Sorry.'

'No, it's alright, I should have called first. Anyway, I thought we could go for a drive. Wee drive on a Sunday, out and about. How do you fancy that?'

'Um, fine. Where are we going? Have you eaten?'

'In reverse order, yes, I have eaten and I thought we should go somewhere, somewhere out west. You don't have to come.'

'What?'

'Ssssh. That time a wee while ago, you were upset . . . The time of the year and all that. Your father. It's like, I never met him. OK? And you don't say that much, right? So. It's very cold, it's not the time of year for it, but I thought we could go to the Garden of Rest. Not if you don't want to. Just a suggestion. You could introduce me. Hm?'

Margaret moved out from the recess and listened to the radio, still chattering in the other room. She perched on a chair arm and wondered how she should feel. Was this a good thing to do? She'd never been back there, not since the funeral. There wasn't a grave she could tend, even if she'd wanted to. Her daddy had been scattered somewhere, maybe already floating in the air as she'd walked back to the black undertaker's car with the strange folding seats, designed to slip back discreetly from people unsteady with grief. She'd hated that about the whole thing – the way that misery had been anticipated, almost rehearsed.

'Margaret, love? Bad idea, eh? Sorry.'

'No, no, I was just in a dwam, thinking.'

'We won't go if it makes you unhappy.'

'Well, it wouldn't make me glad. Sorry, I mean, I'd like to go. It just maybe won't be cheerful. I don't know. You don't mind if I cry.'

'No. It might be good.'

Colin was a great believer in tears. There were times when Margaret noticed they were never *his* tears. Still, he meant well.

The Garden was brittle with frost, beds of indistinguishable shrubs, brown and furred with cold. Under the earth there might be flowers, dead or waiting. The dark, heavy trees had bleached cobwebs laced thickly under their green; a green so dark it was almost black. The grey grass seemed to break beneath their feet.

'Dad. Daddy. His name was Edward. Edward Alisdair Hamilton. I never knew he had a middle name until, well, until it didn't matter.'

'I wish I'd met him. Really. I know he meant a lot to you. I mean, more than most fathers. I know you were very close. The reason I thought we could come here today, I have to take his place.'

'What do you mean?'

'I want to be important to you.'

'Colin, you can't be my father. I'm grown up, I don't even need a father.'

'Do you need anyone?'

'Of course.'

'I need you to be sure about that. I don't want to be wasting my time. I came back for you.'

They were walking arm in arm, hands twisted together and both in Colin's pocket, when Margaret stopped, they both had to. She didn't know whether to be angry or to laugh.

'I don't want to be wasting my time. I don't want to waste yours. I need you, that's all, I need you.'

'I love you.'

'I love you, too. Alright?'

She kissed his nose and then his mouth, freed her hand to close both her arms around him. Their breath came in sheets around them and an elderly couple passed with their heads turned away. Colin and Margaret sat, looking back at their melting footprints from a wooden bench, the winter sun surprisingly piercing.

'What was he called, again?'

'Ted. Well, Edward. Edward Alisdair.'

'OK. Edward Alisdair Hamilton, I'm taking away your daughter now and I hope that we're both very happy.'

'He would want that; for us to be happy.'

'I know. If I have a daughter, I'll be the same.'

'Oh.'

They drove back in the van, Margaret thinking of driving there that time before, when they gave her the privilege of a lonely place in the first car. For the first time, it had occurred to her that she should have tried to find her mother. If she was still alive, she should have been there. Or would Daddy have wanted that?

The car had slid on, Margaret only aware of the stares from the pavement and other cars, of the box in the hearse ahead that held her father. The box she didn't want to follow or think about.

It seemed that everyone knew what to do apart from her. First her father and his box would leave their car and then she could leave hers. For a moment the bier and the undertakers wedged in the door and nobody spoke or laughed or did anything other than smooth away their mistake and slide on. Everything seemed greased, slipping down into death.

The crematorium was full. Daddy had dug people's gardens, had given them flowers, had somehow kept the whole street in a glow of leaves and blossoms, sweet with lavender. And here was the street again with a few lean old men Margaret remembered from the days when her Daddy worked. Men who had come with chairs to be re-upholstered, dealers and suppliers and men who had a strange interest in making wood seem to be old.

Margaret allowed her head to fall. She walked the length of the aisle, not letting the faces catch her eye, not looking at the box, only staring at the glinting bier wheels and the carpet. Her head should be dropped from sadness, but she felt embarrassment, felt the watching faces were testing her grief, pronouncing it inadequate. When she wept it was out of anger. She couldn't sing the hymns, wanted to stay in the rainy Garden, not go back in the sliding car. Some of the faces talked to her and perhaps she spoke back, but she can't remember what she said. She wanted to go home to her Daddy and tell him about it, talk to him.

There was no wake.

As Colin's van moved into the city the sky across the windscreen was almost blinding. The piercing blue with thin, high smears of white made both of them blink. Margaret wiped her eyes.

'You alright, love?'

'Yes, fine now. I'm glad we went. It's very bright, isn't it?'

'Mm hm. Nearly home.'

Margaret was aware that something had changed for Colin

that afternoon. He already seemed more comfortable, self-assured, managing. She didn't feel that anything had changed for her, but perhaps it would happen slowly, perhaps it was on the way. Certainly, it was nice that Colin was happy.

When they reached her flat, Margaret went in alone.

'I understand, you want some time to be on your own.'

'You can come round later.'

'I'll ring first.'

'Aye, OK. You do that.'

'You alright, baby?'

'I'm fine. I feel tired, somehow. But I'm fine. See you later.'

The telephone woke her and she made coffee for when he came in. They went to bed gently, Colin almost paternal, nuzzling her cheek with his day's growth of beard, holding her. Although the room was entirely dark, her new winter curtains keeping the streetlights out, Margaret felt there were times when Colin was looking at her. They lay still and breathed on each other, face to face, and she guessed their eyes were open, reaching for something in the soft black.

Margaret found something in her sleep, something either waiting or brought on by the day. Something not expected.

She stood in a wide, wide room with a blue curving floor which seemed to bend away towards a distance like the surface of a globe. There was an armchair beside her, square-edged, perhaps yellow, and her father sitting in it. He faced forward stiffly into the arc of blue and Margaret was holding his hand.

'Where are you?'

'I'm here. I'm right here.'

'But you're not here with me. I'm on my own. Margaret, I'm on my own. Stay with me.'

'I can't stay.'

'Stay with me.'

'I love you. I do, but I can't stay. I can't be here. I'm not . . . like you. I'm not dead. I would have to be dead to be here. I'm not dead yet.'

'Am I dead?'

She pressed his hand. She had expected it to fade beneath her touch, at least to be cold, but it felt warm and solid. She could feel that there were veins and bones; all the things that a body is made of. There was a pulse.

'Margaret?'

'Yes?'

'If you loved me, you'd be here.'

'I do love you.'

'But you don't understand. You and me, we're the same thing. We're family. We're more than family, we're the same. Two parts of one thing, do you see? And I . . . I love you.'

'Dad.'

'We're the same thing. When I saw you born, living, I knew. We were the same thing. You made a door in me and you got inside, but now I'm empty there. Margaret? Are you here?'

'When it's time, I'll come. I promise. I'll come. I haven't forgotten you. I miss you. I want to talk to you and you're not there. I miss you. We should be in the same place.'

'We are in the same place. You're in me. Like I'm in you.'

'I can't see you. Where are you? Margaret.'

'I'm here. You're just not looking at me. I'm here.'

As she leaned forward to embrace him, she knew he would go away, sink into yellow and then blue.

She woke with the feel of his skin on her neck, his voice in her mind, the softness of his kiss.

'What's the matter? Honey, what's the matter? You're crying.'

Margaret let Colin hold her, knowing she would tell him

nothing because he would not understand and because this had been something private. Family business. Strangely, under the sadness she felt a flicker of peace at that; she was sure she would always be family now, even if nobody else ever knew.

WRIT TO ME

'OK.'

PLEASE

'I will, I promise. OK? There'll be a way.'

'Jamie?'

May flops her magazine down on the table-top.

'Don't annoy Miss Hamilton, now. I'm sure she's had enough of you.'

Irene and May had returned from the buffet car a while before, finding James safely asleep. Irene had taken the seat by the window, keeping her head turned away to the glass. There was something a little discoloured about her face, as if she had been crying or angry. As both women sank behind outstretched magazines there was an air of an argument ended, or at least a truce declared.

'I'm sorry, we didn't mean to be so long away. James kept you entertained?'

There is a rattle from Irene as she turns a page.

'Really, I'm fine. We had a nice time. James was great. Very interesting.'

May smiles, understanding, 'Work with them, do you?'

'I'm sorry?'

'The handicapped.'

'No, no. I mean, sometimes groups came to the place where I worked. We had good access. I mean, they're only people. No, I don't work with them.'

Irene speaks without dipping her magazine.

'We don't work with them, either, dear. We just have them with us, day and night.'

May lets out a tiny breath, too small for a sigh, and then announces, 'We don't really want to talk about this now. We're all a bit tired.' Nobody knows who she means by 'we'.

Margaret and James continue their conversation in silence and whispers, slowly filling another sheet of sugar paper.

WRIT?

Yes.

MISS YOU

Miss you too.

SAD

Yes. I'm sad. Don't worry.

SAD

Around their train brick terraces spin away, bridges and motorways intersect or sway off behind more houses, tangled embankments, sleeper fences and settlements of corrugated workshops. They can't be very far from Warrington.

It was D Day, Minus One. A sign above the café said so. After lunch, Tammy and Gus arrived to see if there was anything they could do and everyone forgot to ask them why they weren't at school. The dominoes players kept to their tables, but their minds were not on the game. Turns were missed and when the sale or return supplies arrived from the Battlefield Bar, all hands abandoned the green baize board and lifted the crates and boxes into the store.

It became quiet, all through the Factory, with work being done. Men and women all wore the same look. The look that came when somebody said that something needed mending, or baking, or digging, or taking in, when somebody needed them: they were being useful. By closing time, everything that could be ready already was and a skittish crowd left the building, as if it had just clocked off.

That evening it was Lesley's turn to lock up so Margaret left the building slightly early, unconcerned by keys. She would have walked directly for the bus-stop, but she heard tentative shuffles and whispers coming from the patch of flattened brick behind the building. Something about the noises was unthreatening so she chose to step loudly round the wall and away from the streetlight, whistling a little.

Balanced along a sunken line of brick she found Elaine, Susan and Tina; pale, their frozen hands clutching them together into a chain. They stared and then slowly crumbled with laughter.

'Fuck, Maggie, we thought you were one of the boys.'

'Nearly killed us. Feel my heart. Feel it.'

Elaine declined Tina's offer and Margaret took the chance to break in.

'What are you doing here anyway? I thought you were a bunch of glue-sniffing axe murderers.'

'Did ye fuck. We're rehearsing, what else would we be doing? And this place fucking stinks, all the old wineys come here to sleep.'

'Smells like they came here to die.'

'So why are you here? Elaine?'

'Because we can't go anywhere else. They won't let us sing up at the school, we couldn't do it in our houses and you won't let us in here.'

'The whole idea was that you took tonight off and had a rest. Your songs are fine, Gus will organise your bit of the evening, he knows the running order. What's the problem?'

'We'll be rotten. We need to rehearse. We'll be terrible. Tina's new man's coming to watch.'

'Shut up.'

'Well, he is.'

'I'm telling him not to come.'

'Are you fuck. I'm wanting a look at his brother.'

'Ladies, you don't need to rehearse. You'll be fine. Just have a bit of confidence, for fuck's sake. You'll be great, steal the show. Now go home and get a rest. And you could knock off the fags for the night, Susan.'

'That'll be right.'

Lesley appeared, one hand deep in her bag and no doubt poised above a can of mace, or something innocent but sharp. She seemed disappointed when she saw the line of girls, but managed to sustain a moderately threatening tone.

'Is everything OK, Maggie?'

'Aye, fine. It's just a troupe of wandering minstrels. Lost wandering minstrels. They're on their way home. No need for the Dobermanns.'

'Have you got a Dobermann, Lesley?'

'I'm allergic to dogs, actually.'

'Oh, she's allergic, actually, girls.'

'Fancy.'

Margaret could see things drifting out of control. Again.

'Come on, we all need to go home. Artistes included.'

They trailed out through the thickening dusk towards the edge of the light from the street.

'Good-night then, girls. I'll see you tomorrow.'

'Aye, maybe.'

'Well, Lesley and I will be there, even if you're not.'

'Go on, Mags, you couldnae manage without us.'

'Even if that was true, do you think I'd tell you?'

'Night Mags.'

'Night, night.'

Margaret turned to Lesley before she could say anything, 'Don't tell me. A spot of abseiling would sort them all out, no problem.'

'Some healthy exercise would certainly do them no harm. If they didn't run a mile at the very thought.'

Margaret smiled when she realised that Lesley hadn't meant to make a joke.

'I could only recommend something I'd be willing to do myself. I leave all that painful, sporting stuff to Colin.'

'Suit yourself. How is he, by the way? We never see him. You should come round. Oh, there's Sammy. Bye. See you tomorrow. Bye.'

'Goodbye, Lesley.' Margaret watched her disappear into Sam's old Vauxhall, relieved they hadn't thought to offer her a lift.

Margaret didn't expect to be back at the Factory later that night. She had settled herself for an early night, bathed, slipped into bed and was on the edge of sleeping when the phone rang.

'What are you wearing?'

'What? Colin?'

'What are you wearing?'

'I'm in bed. I was asleep. Nearly.'

'So what are you wearing?'

'Nothing. Obviously. I don't wear anything in bed.'

'I know.'

'I know you know. Is this leading anywhere?'

'Come out with me. Get dressed and come out.'

'Colin.'

'Please. I need to talk to you.'

'Then come round and talk.'

'No. We need to be out, it's a lovely night.'

'Are you alright?'

'Of course.'

'You haven't taken anything?'

'Oh, for Christ's sake, just come out. Look I'll be round in about fifteen minutes, if you're there, you're there. If you're not, I'll go away again.'

'If I'm where?'

'Outside. I'll see you. Bye.'

Margaret rolled on to her back, thinking that Colin always did this. He would suddenly have a wild idea, entirely unreasonable, but if she tried to say a thing about it, he would get hurt and she would feel entirely unreasonable and then guilty and then he would get his own way. Always. Not that she didn't appreciate the odd wild idea; they were nice, the kind of things women appreciated in romantic novels. He just had such rotten timing. Inconsiderate. She had half a mind not to go out. Why should she wait outside for him at nearly twelve o'clock when she had a very busy day ahead, followed by a long night? She would do it anyway, of course. Despite herself.

Was this her growing up and getting sensible, or getting old and set in her ways?

Was this him off his head again?

There was a wind scuttling along the kerb as she moved down the steps to the pavement. In a few hours the frost would be forming, when the clouds had passed and the air was still.

Colin pulled up in the company van, just as Margaret started to shiver.

'There you are.'

'This is where you said you wanted me to be.'

'Aye, but you sounded pretty grumpy, you know?'

'I always am when I've just woken up.'

'Aye right. Buckle up, now, seat-belts on and safety first.'

He took the corner at the end of the road in fourth.

'Why is it whenever you talk about safety I feel at risk?'

'Paranoia, hen, just paranoia. What's the point of driving carefully at night? In the daytime, I could understand. You've seen me, Mr Clean.'

'Well, at night, it's Mr Hyde.'

'Are you going to nip my head all night, or will I start steering with my knees?'

'No, you will not.'

'Only on the straight bits, I do it all the time.'

'I wish I thought you didn't. This isn't your van.'

'Precisely, lighten up.'

They slithered out along the dual carriageway, overtaking a touch too early, or maybe a touch too late, something risky about the feel of the wheels beneath them.

'Nights like this, I wish I was American. They have roads you can really drive on. I used to try this round London – not a bloody hope. At least you can hit the countryside up here. We're going to the countryside tonight, but not just yet. First things first, as old Archie used to say. Guess where we're going.'

'I have no idea.'

'Aye, you do. Come on. We're following the bus route.'

'The bus? Oh no. You're not. It's bad enough in daylight.'

'You guessed. The Fun Factory. A little visit and then we move on. Geez a wee feel of your body, while I'm at it. That bit. Go on, if I have to look for it, I'll need to take my eyes off the road. Oh, there it was, all the time.'

'Where did you expect?'

'Things change.'

But the Factory was just the same. Apparently even grubbier in the dark, with a greasy sheen of cold over its walls.

'Prepare to steam windows.'

The van nosed into the corner away from the light and on to the old brick, parked where the girls had been trying to sing. There was no one there now.

'What are you doing?'

'I wanted to talk.'

'Really.'

'Come here first, though.'

Afterwards Margaret would wonder why they had done that, making love in a van on a patch of waste ground, something from the seat-belt nipping her back. Why do it like that, the way they'd never had to? As if they were hiding out from their parents? As if Colin was paying her; a commercial one-night stand? As if they'd both had another wild idea?

'Thanks.' Colin wriggled back into his seat.

'No trouble.'

'No, I mean, I know it's bit weird, alright. I know. I get nervous and I don't know what else to do.'

'I see. I don't know if that's entirely complimentary, you know? You said you wanted to talk. Did I have to be subdued first, shagged into submission?'

'You didn't like it?'

'Liked it fine. I don't know why it happened, that's all. Not that I always need a why. What is it. Why are you nervous? What's the matter? Hm?'

'Hang on, I'll get us out of here. The country bit. If I stick to my timetable, I'll be fine. No bother. You alright?'

'I don't know what you're talking about, but otherwise, I'm fine.'

The dark cooried in round the windows as they left the streetlights and turned down into lanes. Fractions of trees and stone wall drew up alongside them and flicked out and Margaret followed the tunnel of light ahead, feeling somehow cosy.

'Do you want some music on?'

'Is that a hint?'

'Not at all, I thought it might relax you. Tell me, come on.'

'Alright. It's nothing much. That is, I don't know how much it is. I feel that something happened a while ago. We seemed to

164

pass a point, I don't know, I just felt that something should have happened, a change.'

'You want me to change?'

'No. Not especially.

'It's the way we are, you see. There are times when I feel, there are things we're not doing. It's been more than two years since I came back, since we've been together, and there are things we don't do. Maybe we never will, but we don't talk about them. I don't know if they're possible. I mean, could I ask you something?'

'Of course. Ask.'

The van rode on, its light bumping ahead, its engine the only noise they were aware of.

'Go on. Ask me. I don't bite. You're the one that bites.'

'Sorry.'

'Not at all, please go on.'

'Aye, well, OK. I just wondered if you would think about living with me, with a view to doing something else. I mean, I'd like to marry you. I'd like to make this serious. Because I'm serious.'

'So am I.'

'Good, good. Just think about it. No deadline, nothing demanding. I know I can be demanding.'

'I was about to say. You were pretty keen on getting the keys to my flat.'

'You've got the keys to mine.'

'Yes, I do. Look, this is very flattering. Apart from anything else. Definitely. But I will have to think. Don't be offended. I'm not saying no. It's more that I don't know how to do it.'

'Well, we can work that out. Sorry. Sorry, not rushing you, just a suggestion. You know me, I'm all for forward motion. Standing still worries me.'

'Yeah. Will we have a nice drive home now? I'll put in a tape. Do you fancy holding hands around your gearstick.'

'Any time. Any time.'

The morning was clear and very frosty and Margaret was less tired than she'd expected. Colin had trouble starting the van.

Margaret found Graham on the doorstep when she came to unlock.

'I don't even wake up this early to sign on.'

'You could have had a wee lie in, it's not as if nearly everything isn't done. You look a bit rough.'

'You're not kidding. See, it occurred to me that there is a class of bastard who would see all that booze going in there a day early and decide to rip us off. You know? So I've been keeping an eye on the place.'

'What, all night?'

'Only on and off. Don't look so worried, Maggie, it was no bother. To tell the truth, the woman came back and put me out again, so it made a break from sleeping up my own close. Come down here and be useful. You know, I've just realised, she never puts me out when it's fucking warm.'

'Did you see anything?'

'Me? Naw. Quiet all night. Too cold for anything to happen.'

'I suppose so.'

Just before the lunchtime rush, Mr Lawrence marched from his office to the café counter. The room focused its concentration intently on newspapers, dominoes, coffee-stains, boots, anything that wasn't Mr Lawrence.

Mr Lawrence tapped a fork on the formica counter. The

silence became more silent and, as Margaret and Lesley emerged from the office, he began.

'Ladies and gentlemen, as you all know, tonight there will be a fund-raising ceilidh on these premises. Something I'm sure we will all enjoy in good spirit. We'll have fun and I'm sure we will all have nothing to reproach ourselves with in the morning.

'I would draw your attention to the special support this project has received from a member of our own staff, Margaret Hamilton. You all probably know that I am not generous with my praise, but I think we would all agree that this is another job well done. Thank you for your help, Margaret.'

Even with both eyes on the ground, Margaret knew he was looking at her.

It's time for James to go now. Warrington is almost here, the train slowing too slightly to be noticed, then a little more and then a little more. A narrow rain is waiting to meet it.

May has gone to fetch the guard and Irene has almost finished clearing the table-top. The paper and markers disappear, James too late to catch them. His games of noughts and crosses, conversations, observations, brief asides, are folded into the carrier bag reserved for rubbish and scraps. He eases his head round to Margaret, hands clasped close to his chest.

'Well, James Watt. Nearly time for you to go. I'm sorry you're not coming all the way. Take care of yourself.'

James extends a hand forward to be shaken.

'Thanks, James. Thanks.'

All along the carriage, bags and cases are reached out or lifted down, coats are smoothed and put on, but James is still looking at Margaret, unable to be precise about any message because he has no precise way to pass one on. He looks and holds Margaret's hand, looks away. He has eyes which are very pleasantly blue. She hadn't noticed that before.

They all watch the station give a tiny jolt beside them and come to a halt. The carriage slowly clears enough for May and the guard to move along it and make themselves ready for James. Irene slips out and settles her bags on the table.

'You can bet he'll need changing.'

May smiles at Margaret as she loosens James's hand away, neatly arranges the wheelchair to receive him. Margaret, her hands free now, tears off a corner from her paper, begins to write.

'Well, it's been a long journey. Nice to have met you, dear. Hope we've not disturbed you too much.'

'No, not at all. I wondered, this is my address. If James wanted to write, if he wanted me to write to him . . .'

Irene is already on the platform, surrounded by bags. She is looking along the platform at something Margaret cannot see.

'That's very nice of you dear, but you really mustn't.'

'I would like to.'

'Really, no.'

The buckles are all in place around James and his chair, a blanket being eased up around him. Margaret pushes the corner of paper into his hand as it disappears.

'There, now James has my address. I really would like to keep in touch. We seem to have made friends.'

'Well, we'll see, dear. You have to understand, Irene isn't the only one who's disappointed. James gets disappointed, too. He gets let down.'

James lets out a fragment of sound and fumbles under his blanket. His eyes stay on Margaret.

'Just you keep nicely tucked in, son, it's cold out there and you know what you're like with the cold.'

'Goodbye, James. I'll not shake your hand again. I *can't* shake your hand. Goodbye, then.'

For no reason she understands, Margaret leans and kisses

James, just reaching his forehead above one eye. This seems the right thing to do.

'Right, well, we'll not hold up the train any longer.' And James is lifted down and away. Margaret waves. A hand struggles out of the blanket to wave back, letting a piece of paper fall and blow along the platform out of sight.

Margaret finds she has a tightness in her throat as the carriage edges into movement. She cannot settle to read.

The Fisherman's Ceilidh is a memory now, kept safe in Margaret's mind. When she thinks of it, it birls the way a ceilidh always should, almost as shining and moving as the night when her father danced.

In the dark, the Factory door was propped half open, a slab of interior light laid flat across the path. Someone was playing a record of Jimmy Shand and the music was edging out into the frost above the sound of voices. Seven o'clock.

'*Courage, mes braves* and here we go. Nae booze for the barmen, nae tick on any terms. But the stovies and the oatcakes are all free.'

Margaret stepped into a room she couldn't recognise. Within the last two hours there had been changes. A huge man in a kilt ground past her, quietly adamant.

'There's nothing wrong with Jimmy Shand, he's a grand wee man.'

'Dougie, pal, he's mince. I mean, have you ever seen him playing? He's a miserable old sod. That's not an accordion wrapped round him, it's a bloody iron lung.'

'I suppose you don't like Alisdair Gillies, either.'

Graham, suddenly dapper in a blue serge suit, moved from

group to group dispensing his final advice. He looked younger without his bunnet. Even slightly magical.

'Coffin Maggie and her man are barred for reasons you can guess and so is Bobby The Dug if he brings his punchbowl. We're having none of that.'

Margaret stared at the Factory; it was transformed. The walls and ceiling were looped with tartan cloth: ribbons, blankets, scarves, whole bolts of something broad and mainly brown. A battered Saltire was fixed above the PA. And on any available surface there were signs: new signs, handwritten in broad black on wide sheets of lining paper. Each was a quotation, neatly marked with its author's name: Thoreau, Brecht, Paine, Thomas Muir, Cervantes.

'Any problems, look for me. Any serious bother, then look for Big Douglas, your man in the kilt. Aye, what is it hen?'

Margaret stood very still. Reading.

' "My equals burst but once upon the world and their first stroke displays their mastery." '

Graham smiled, 'Pierre Corneille, from *The Cid*, whit else would you put on your wall? Och, would you look at that poor bugger.'

Sammy was sunk in a chair near the Blue Room, his guitar pulled close to his chest. 'He's been tuning and retuning since he came, either that or staring into space. I don't think a paying audience is entirely his cup of tea.'

'Graham, this is all very nice, but why do you have Corneille on your wall, why anyone?'

'To make the night complete. Food, bevvy, music, singing, dancing, all of that, but there's got to be something there for your brain, for your soul. When folk sing the songs, they don't always think what they're saying. That's the Scottish Problem; we're aye fucking singing, but what do we ever hear?'

'You're off your head, you know that?'

'There's no other way to be. Look over there – René Descartes. His "Second Meditation", fucking read it. He's telling me I can be everything, the whole fucking world – telling me that I can do that. I have that inside. And I'm fed up with folk who are certain that I'm nothing but shite underfoot. Tonight, I'm backing Descartes. We all are.'

'Graham?'

'Aye?'

'I like the signs. You're still off your head, but I like them and I'll tell you something nice that makes me like them even more. Lawrence will fucking hate every single one. His bulgy wee eyes will finally leave his bulgy wee fucking head.'

'Strong language suits you, you know that?'

Margaret laughed and then shivered a little.

'Aye, maybe.'

'Well, you can do us all a favour, while you're on a roll. Go and persuade Big Dougie to leave the record selection to somebody sane. If he carries on with this shite, the boys'll make up a menoge to fucking gub him.' He held her shoulder gently, 'No, no, stay here. I'm only kidding. And I've got a wee announcement to make.' He stepped on to a swaying, plastic chair. 'Ladies and gents you've been entirely wonderful. Less of that fucking music while I'm talking! Thanks. This'll be a good night and we'll have made it that way. But you'll not mind me asking a wee cheer for Maggie here. For all her help. For – she's – a – jolly – good – fellow – '

'Och, Graham.'

'We wouldn't forget you, Maggie, even if you'd like us to.'

Outside, the bridge across the canal was beginning to shine with frost. There was a thin mist on the water, no movement beneath. Everything as Margaret had left it before she came in. She had looked down and seen a small moon, deep in the cold water, a smirr of orange streetlight, but no sign of herself, not even a shadow.

For a moment, she was almost afraid. There came a feeling that somebody might be behind her; that a reflection might fall on the water, showing her own face and then another. She felt colder than the night should make her.

'Daddy?'

Her whisper floated down and off the bridge, caught in a little breeze, thin and white. Margaret thought of the place where her father was now: the black green trees and the frost grey grass. She couldn't imagine him in the earth, nor in anything other than the present tense.

'I can't be dancing with you. Not tonight. But I'll dance for you.'

The little moon was a painful white as she looked up, like a hole in the sky, leading through to a very bright room.

'You said I should live Dad. Everything else is a waste of time. You told me. A waste of time.'

She waited for a while, trying to hear a noise from the dead water.

'But all I do is waste my time. How am I supposed to do anything else? Nobody told me. You never said a word and we're family, remember?'

It is the only time she recalls being angry with her father. She put her hands on the burning cold of the metal handrail and wanted to hit it, to hit him. And then his face came clearer in her mind than she had seen it since he left her and she knew she couldn't hurt it, couldn't let it alter under any kind of pain. Her sigh misted over the bridge and down.

'I know it's nobody's fault. I know that. It was just, we ran out of time. I wish we hadn't. It makes me angry. I'd have told you things. If you'd been here I would have let you know things. Like, I can breathe fire. I learned how to do that. And other things. There are lots of things you didn't know I could do. Lots of things you thought I could.'

A wave slapped against brickwork and she noticed her hands were throbbing. She thought of slipping them flat against her father's back and rubbing her chin into his shoulder as if they were going to start a slow dance. As if they were going to stand that way for ever.

Margaret saw Colin before he noticed her. He was sitting with his head bent forward, polishing glasses. Heather nudged his elbow, pointed, and he turned. He smiled. He smiled a smile entirely for Margaret. A broad, broad grin.

It always surprised her somehow, when Colin was so pleased, so easily; when he answered the phone, quite formal but polite, and then heard her voice and changed and warmed in the space of a word. It was almost painful to think of. Now, before she knew it, they were both smiling, almost laughing, and then walking to the point where they would meet.

'Geez a kiss.'

'What kind would you like?'

'I don't know, let me try one.'

There was a time, around twenty past eight, when it seemed the thing would never get started. One of the dominoes players sat and waited at the door beside a table full of tickets and stacks of change. A few couples straggled in and then hid themselves in the bar. The rooms seemed cold and too brightly lit. Margaret sat beside Colin against the wall, watching nothing happen, and then they came.

As if a queue had been forming somewhere out in the dark, or a coach had arrived, as if an agreed time had been reached, in the people came. Within fifteen minutes the air was hot and poisonous with cigarette smoke, hoarse with noise; the bar staff were surrounded and the first turn was on.

Mr and Mrs Lawrence appeared, rather quietly, while a duo sang and played the spoons. One of the singers confessed the spoons were a recent innovation and somewhere a shout broke through.

'You could have been playing they things for years, it's the singing that's shite.'

The Lawrences were locked in, side by side, as if their arms had been sewn together in some terrible accident. Their lips moved while their faces stared out at the crowd. Perhaps they were shouting; nobody could hear them, if they were. They struggled apart and left the room through separate doors. Mr Lawrence returned with two plates of stovies, found himself a seat then draped his coat across another. He waited for a while, then ate his stovies and waited again. A man came and sat on his coat, leaning forward and clapping his hands while a fiddler played jigs and reels. When the man pointed to the other plate of stovies, Lawrence gave them him and turned to the sign beside them both. He might have been reading it, although from a distance it seemed that his eyes were closed.

In the front office, by special permission, the Youth Theatre was drinking cider and telling itself it shouldn't be drinking cider, not at its age. It worried its way quietly through rows of glasses, lines of songs. When Margaret opened the door, Susan gave a small scream.

'What's the matter?'

'I'm gonny die and no one believes me.'

'That's a shame. Will you manage to do a wee gig before the interment?'

'You don't believe me either.'

'Just ignore her, Maggie. She's been dying all fucking day.' Gus leaned back in his chair, feet propped across a drawer extending from Margaret's desk. He tapped his cigarette ash into a matchbox. Maggie winked at him.

'Well, in that case you'll all be very glad to know that this is your five-minute call. I suggest, because the place is packed with adoring crowds, that you come out now with your hands up and try to work your way towards the stage.'

'What does that mean?'

'It means you're on.'

The room was already scrambling up, adjusting, clearing its throat. Tam, luminous with aftershave, dipped his head down to kiss Margaret as he led the way past and through the door. Margaret then found herself kissed by all the boys and hugged or pecked professionally by the girls.

'Break a leg.

'Good luck.

'You'll be great.

'Good luck.

'Good luck.'

She felt as if she were witnessing a strange kind of parachute jump as their line moved off, pushing into the smoke and darkness, the bars of light. Onstage, a friend of Heather's was delivering 'The Flowers Of The Forest' with bursts on a militant guitar. Margaret closed the front-office door and waited.

Gus and Tam had sprung to the microphone before the last turn's final chord had clattered into place.

'Good evening, ladies and gentlemen, this part of the evening's entertainment will be provided by your friendly neighbourhood

Youth Theatre and, without further ado, I would like to recite for you some old and greatly respected Scottish verse, taught to me by my old and greatly respected grandfather. I would ask for your silence and attention, this is a very sad poem; indeed, a yearning lament for all the lost glories of the bens and glens, the purple heather and the Famous Grouse. Ladies and gentlemen, I give you "The Effan Bee".'

Heads appeared from the Blue Room, lipsticked mouths were pursed and Bobby The Dug's Other Sister suddenly laughed like a cat sliding down a hot fence. Margaret felt her hands unclench.

'There you are.' Colin slipped his arms around her, just above the waist. 'The team's doing alright, eh?'

'Taught them everything they know.'

'I don't think I'd admit to that, if I were you. I'm starved, do you want some oatcakes and stuff, they've run out of stovies.'

'Alright, I'll just stay and watch them, though. If you don't mind. And don't do that.'

'What?'

'That. Someone will see.'

'Nobody's looking. And who cares if they do see? I'm not ashamed.'

'Neither am I, love, but I'm technically on duty. I don't think that's meant to include getting groped.'

'I'll get your oatcakes.'

'Hang on and give us a kiss, though.'

'No, I'll not embarrass you at your work.'

'Colin.'

'What?'

'When are you singing?'

'I don't know, when Graham tells me.'

Colin left her to watch while Tam joined Gus to sing 'Three Men Fae Carntyne' and 'Hot Ashphalt'. The choruses from the floor were relaxed and willing, sliding gently into incapacitation. Bobby The Dug's Other Sister was still laughing.

He took me for a picnic, doon by the Rouken Glen,
He showed tae me the bonnie wee birds and he showed me a bonnie
wee hen.
'Oh God, is he no gorgeous. Him in the leather jacket. The wee one with the nice eyes.'
He showed tae me the bonnie wee birds fae the lintie tae the
craw,
'If I was twenty years younger.'
Then he showed tae me the bird that stole my thingumyjig awa'.
'He'd no huv been born, pet, dinny upset yoursel.'

The boys finished strongly, refusing all encores, and Gus led on Toaty Boady. Colin slid back with two plates.
'Prepare to see grown men cry and here's your oatcakes.'
'What?'
'Here's your oatcakes.'
'Thanks. Oh, fuck.'
'Now what?'
'Lawrence, I can see him behind your shoulder. He's waving me over. I don't want to speak to him now. Not now.'
'Pretend you haven't seen him.'
'He'll only come and get me. Hold my oatcakes, I'll be back. Colin?'
'Aye?'
'If I'm not, come and get me.'
'Sure. Of course. Sure.'

Mr Lawrence waited, rubbing one hand across his face, as if he really wished it would go away.

'Margaret. I do apologise for this. I really wouldn't involve you if I didn't have to. This is difficult. I – '

Lawrence seemed to forget he had been speaking, his eyes wavering over something beyond Margaret's shoulder. When she spoke he gave a slight start.

'There's something you want me to do.'

'Oh. Yes. Ah, no, not want. I need you to do something. I don't want it at all. Can I trust you?'

'Well, yes.'

'Good. Good. I hoped I could. The ladies' lavatory, I can't go in. My wife, you see, she has been in the ladies' lavatory for quite some time now and I – There is a possibility she could be ill. Would you?'

'What, you want me to go in and check how she is? You're sure she's in there?'

'That would be quite difficult to say. I believe she is. If you could. Her first name is Daisy. Sometimes, I find, she doesn't answer to "Mrs Lawrence". Daisy.'

'Fine, OK.'

'Great. My turn to apologise. Really. There was no one else I could ask.'

He walked slowly into the crowd, saying something Margaret couldn't hear.

There were only two cubicles in the ladies'. Margaret pushed the first door gently and it swung in, bouncing slightly when it hit the wall. Nobody home. The sudden quiet made her ears ring. It was cold, almost clammy. And then she recognised the perfume. Someone behind the second door had that peculiar smell of perfume and decay now mixed with a new, oily sweetness.

'Mrs Lawrence? I mean, Daisy? Are you there? Are you alright?'

There was breathing coming from the cubicle, quite deep and slow, as if the person might be asleep. At least she was alive.

'Mrs – Daisy, if you're in any difficulty, I'm sure we can help. There's no need to be embarrassed.' The breathing continued a slow beat. 'Are you awake? Are you alright?'

Margaret backed away slowly, hoping she would be able to see beneath the door; a sign of something, water, blood. Her feet were very loud on the linoleum.

'Is there something I can help you with?'

'If you like.' The voice from the cubicle was deep and slurring.

'Oh. Oh, good, you're there. How can I help?'

'You could strangle my husband.'

'I'm sorry.'

'Oh don't be that. You want to help me, you can strangle my husband.' There was an odd laugh and a shifting of feet.

'Would that help?'

'Of course it wouldn't help, you silly cunt. Of course it wouldn't help, nothing will help. Fucking help. Did I *ask* for fucking help. No. I *ask* you, I *ask* you to strangle my husband. Because it would make me enormously happy.' Again the laugh.

'I'll just go and tell him you're alright. You are alright? I'll just go and tell him how you are. I'll be back, I'll be right back.'

'Don't expect him to be surprised, hinny, don't expect that. And come back with a drink. I need a fucking drink. Easier. You bring me a little bottle and you won't need to run about. A big bottle. You see I'm very thirsty, but I don't feel well, so I can't come out just now. Whisky's the best when I'm not well. Don't listen to that wee shite. Whisky's the best. Thank you dear, I know you'll help me. You understand.'

Colin was waiting outside in the corridor.

'What's the matter? Has that little prick said something to you?'

'No, no, look – '

A blonde-haired woman was heading for the toilet door.

'I'm sorry, you can't go in there.'

'Whit?'

'You can't go in there.'

'And where else am I supposed to go?'

'Well, could you be quick.'

'Whit?'

'Nothing, nothing. That's fine. If you take the one nearest the door, that's fine, that's fine.'

A pale back, almost concealed in blue satin was already disappearing into the empty cubicle.

'I wouldny go in the other one, would I? I'm no gonny sit on her lap.'

Margaret tugged Colin's sleeve.

'Come over here. Mrs Lawrence is in there. She's totally pissed and locked in a cubicle. Lawrence asked me to find out how she was. He must have known how she fucking was. I can only assume that this makes it my fault. Now I'll have to go and tell him. Could you stand here and listen. In case anything happens? Thanks. You're very good to me.'

'I know.'

Lawrence was sitting very close by the door, watching Toaty Boady, or rather watching the lines of backs between him and her voice. As Margaret moved towards him, heads turned aside, there were coughs and sniffs. She brushed behind Mr Ho, his face smiling and bathed in tears. Big Douglas towered above a press of dark suits, head back, eyes closed. The whole audience was tensing against the onset of emotion and then slowly giving way. Toaty Boady made them want to give way.

'Mr Lawrence.'

'I saw you coming. She's still in there, isn't she. She won't come home.'

'She is in there, yes, and she didn't mention coming home.'

'Drunk.'

'I think so.'

'Don't be ridiculous. You think so. How obvious does it need to be. Thank you for saving my feelings, but in this case I have none to save. Not there any more.'

The look Lawrence gave her, made Margaret catch her breath. It was wild, almost hungry, unwillingly confined. Margaret cleared her throat.

'I haven't even seen her. She's locked in a cubicle. She sounds very drunk. She sounds upset.'

'Did she give you any message?'

'No. No, she didn't.'

'I see. Not like her to be shy. I would like you to tell her that I'm leaving in twenty minutes and I hope to take her with me. If I cannot remove her, someone else will have to. That may mean the police. We're getting used to that. She has twenty minutes.'

'Well, I'll do my best.'

'And Margaret?'

'Yes?'

'You understand, don't you?'

'I, I don't think – '

He leant very close.

'I seem to have developed a rather limited social life, emotional life. I didn't want it to be like this. I simply seem never to get what I *do* want. I appreciate your efforts.'

'Um, that's alright. That's no bother. Twenty minutes.'

'You give me hope, sometimes. I didn't expect that.'

'Mr Lawrence?'

'See what you can do.'

He forced out his hand to shake hers, pushing her back to arm's length and then held her by the wrist until it hurt.

'See what you can do for me.'

Toaty Boady's voice was flickering above them now, clearer than a soul, bright and beyond reach. Around the room, the staring, blinking, fluttering eyes saw a collier's boy, bodies felt his chill in their bones and minds were almost at the place where they would act, where they would make a move to somehow save him. When Toaty Boady finished, they would still be at the edge, then they would topple back and be safe, come to very quietly. Perhaps slightly changed. Margaret felt uneasy, forcing her way through such intent bodies.

'Colin?'

Colin was standing with his back to the door of the ladies', tears rolling down to his chin. He looked round at Margaret and smiled.

'She's wonderful, isn't she. Fucking amazing.'

'Have you heard anything.'

'No, no, nothing at all. The blonde came out, that's all. Fucking amazing singer, that wean. Kiss me.'

'Aye, OK. Look, I have to go in there for a bit, alright? And don't let anyone else come in here.'

'Whit?'

'Well try your best.'

Margaret went to the bar and bought a half-pint of diluting orange juice, then she went into the toilet and slid it under the second cubicle door.

'Where the fuck have you been?' The glass disappeared. 'I suppose this is a joke. My husband's idea of a joke.'

'I don't know what you mean.'

'This fucking piss.' There was the sound of a liquid being poured into more liquid. 'Get me a drink.'

'Your husband sent a message.'

'Get me a fucking drink. Drink, then the message. That's the rules.'

'If I get you a drink, you have to go with your husband in twenty minutes. More like fifteen minutes now.'

'I didn't hear that. I can't hear until I've had a drink. Rules.'

Margaret came back with a whisky and water, slid it under the door. The half-pint glass was already down there, full of a cloudy yellow liquid.

'Now you can take the other glass away.'

'No.'

'Sorry, that's the rules. Or no message. In fact, take both the fucking glasses away.'

An emptied tumbler was set down on the linoleum. Margaret lifted it away to the shelf above the sink.

'Both glasses. That's the rules.'

Margaret picked up the other glass. It was warm, wet, the liquid inside had a chemical smell. She emptied the glass in the other toilet then ran it and her hands under the tap.

'Both empty. Satisfied?'

'No, why should I be?'

'Why should you be? I'll tell you why you fucking should be. Because no human being should have to do what I've just done. Why don't you piss on the floor, if you have to, like any other fucking animal? I don't have to slop out for you. I don't even know you. I don't even want to be here. Why don't you just fuck off with your fucking husband. Whatever your problem is with him, it's none of my bloody business.'

'You alright in there?'

'Aye, Colin, fine. Mrs Lawrence is just teaching me some points of etiquette.'

Now, from inside the cubicle, there was crying. Long, heavy sobs.

'Oh, for fuck's sake. Colin, go and get a whisky, a double. It's fine, just go and get one.'

Colin left and the sobs continued.

'Do you really want to finish the night drunk and crying in a toilet.'

'No, I don't. I don't want anything. I want to die.'

'Wait till you start to sober up, things will seem better. It's always worse at night.'

'What the fuck do you know?'

'Nothing. I just think you deserve better. Anyone would. Come on out. Someone's bringing you a whisky, but you'll have to come out.'

'No tricks.'

'There's a whisky coming, but you have to be out.'

Inside the cubicle feet skidded, something fell against the door, pulled back and the crying continued. Almost five minutes passed before the door jerked open and Margaret and Colin slid forward to catch Mrs Lawrence. She didn't look good.

'OK, Daisy, we're going to get you outside to the car. You're doing fine.'

'Where's the fucking whisky.'

'Try and do without it.'

'Fuck you.' She twisted wildly in their arms.

'Alright, alright, you'll get it.'

They held her upright from either side while Margaret held the glass to her lips. Daisy spilled some of the whisky, too anxious to swallow, choking it down.

Out in the room, Elaine was singing 'Come On Baby Light My

Fire' and Daisy was pressed through the crowd, the almost solid, sticky air, with hardly a murmur of notice. Outside the night was icy and bitter with the exhaust smoke pluming from Lawrence's car. Daisy vomited.

Lawrence pushed his head out of the driver's window. 'Is she coming?'

'I'd rather fucking walk.'

'No, Daisy, you'll be better off in the car with your husband. You can't walk.'

'Of course I can fucking walk. I just needed to be sick. Fucking stovies. Make anyone sick.'

'Is she coming?'

Daisy shook her props away, took a step and fell.

'I'm fine, I'm fine. Ice everywhere. Fuck! Get back, you cunts, I'm not a fucking cripple!' She scrambled up and lunged towards the car, kicked it, almost falling, and leant forward to walk again, shouting to no one in particular, 'You know why I married the little fuck? I knew he'd make me drink, I fucking knew he'd make me drink.'

Margaret stepped forward from the doorway. 'Mr Lawrence, do you want us to help her into the car.'

'Does he fuck!'

'Mr Lawrence?' But Lawrence had already opened his door and grabbed his wife from behind. She fell again, or perhaps was overbalanced, and he dragged her by the arm to the passenger's door, opened it and punched her in. She screamed and laughed alternately as he locked the door.

Lawrence stood, his face white and open in the dark, wiping his hands on his jacket sleeves, panting. A pale hand flared towards Margaret and then fell.

'You'll dance with me, Margaret, when I come back. You'll do that for me?'

He smiled, his eyes making two neat spaces through and into the night.

It's odd in the train without James. The carriage windows seem to have run out of countryside and Margaret watches one dull town smirr into another. When they pass into sun the graffiti she sees by the track is unfamiliar, definitely English now. A foreign country opens ahead and then closes behind her and she can imagine the white light on the lines, pushing all the way to London on her behalf.

A thick black marker pen was left on James's seat. Now it is in Margaret's pocket; something she feels she will keep to remind her of a friend.

DIFFRENT

'Yes, but I still don't understand that.'

NO ME

'How can you not be you?'

EASY

'Actually, now you say it, yes. I do it all the time.'

NOW?

'No, not now.'

?

'Because — '

???

'Alright, alright. Because it's different on trains. I was told. Worries on board and off they go without you. They go on ahead, or in the guard's van or something. I was told. I mean, you can relax here – this isn't anywhere. Whatever happens outside, there's nothing we can do about it right now. And you meet people that – '

Margaret remembers that she stopped herself from saying they were people you would never see again; that it didn't matter what you told them. She wanted to see James again. That was important.

PEOPLE CAN TALK TO

She had the impression he wrote that very quickly, as if he were hurrying to save her from embarrassment. The way a friend would.

PEOPLE CAN TALK TO

'Yes. You meet people you can talk to and be yourself with. Not often, but you do. Are you yourself now?'

YES NO PILLS NO JAGS ALL MEEEE

'One-hundred per cent James Watt. I'm honoured.'

FUC

'Away you go. You should learn to take compliments better, then you'll get more.'

FUC WON HUNNER PERCEN MEEEEEE

Which was all that seemed to matter at the time. She hopes no one manages to change that.

As Margaret and Colin walked back to the ceilidh the grind of Lawrence's car was fading along the road, Bobby The Dug waved his arm and smiled.

'Only God can make a tree. Eh? Only God can make a tree.'

He nodded until his glasses began to slither down his nose, then sat at rest, smiling and certain another thought would come. A good one.

Graham stepped up quietly and took Margaret's arm. She continued to walk, slung uncomfortably between the two men.

'Bit of bother?'

She pulled them to a stop and freed herself before she answered.

'Mrs Lawrence seemed to be upset about something. Possibly her life. Colin and I passed her on to Mr Lawrence. He was upset, too. I think I'm upset, if anyone's interested. I think I'm upset.'

Margaret walked to the back office, turned on the light and went in. Almost as soon as she sat and closed her eyes, a knock came at the door. She knew it would be Colin.

'Can I come in?'

'Sure, sure. Just don't expect me to make any sense. Did you see his face. Christ. How the hell do you think they survive? I'd go mad.'

'Maybe they have.'

'And Lawrence wants me in there somewhere. Holding his hand. Whatever. He wants to add me into that.'

'Do you want to cry?'

'No, I do not want to fucking cry. I'm fucking angry. Fucking angry. I should have done something. We should have. But what is there you can do?'

'Well they deserve each other.'

'No they don't. They don't deserve that. Nobody does.'

'It's alright.'

'No it's not.'

'We're alright. We can't do anything about it. That's up to them. We're alright. Aren't we alright?'

'Yes. Yes, we're alright.' She slid her fingers between his. 'I think that's what makes it worse when other people aren't. We're alright. No problem.'

When Colin sang that night, Margaret could still feel the pressure of his fingers between hers. His aftershave was in her hair and on her neck. He seemed to be going down well, heads around him swayed, feet keeping time softly, beating like a fragmented heart. Whenever Margaret heard him she was surprised that his voice wasn't deeper; he looked to her as though he would have a deeper voice. But it was soft and light, seeming to carry almost in spite of itself. There was a moment when she felt his eyes find her among the other faces, she smiled a little and looked away, realising she felt quite proud, in fact, very proud.

There was a tug on Colin's arm as he moved to join Margaret. He turned and saw a neat, slim man with an oddly bright smile. The man extended a hand for shaking.

'How do you do?'

'Fine, great, hello.'

'You're Colin McCoag.'

'Could well be. Who's asking?'

'Nobody. I was merely confirming an assumption. I'm very pleased to meet you, Colin McCoag. You have a good voice – distinctive, like your face.'

'Thanks, but I'm not giving up the day job.'

The man continued to stare at Colin, continued to grip his hand, quite firmly. Colin shivered him off.

'I think I've already said thanks. And now, I have someone waiting for me. I'm going to join them.'

'Of course, so sorry to have detained you. I just enjoy meeting people, can't get enough of it. Cheerio. See you.'

When Colin and the man with the perfect teeth meet again, there will only be a flicker of familiarity, of old dreams, which Colin will ignore.

Graham had taken the floor now, introducing Mr Ho, and Colin fetched Margaret to ease her near the front so they could both smile their support. Mr Ho, gleaming and dumpy, released a deep, warm croon. He snuggled up to the microphone, hands held forward in supplication, and delivered a medley of Crosby and Sinatra hits. The room sang along, rippling slightly with each communal breath. Margaret pinched Colin hard on the arm when she discovered he was giggling.

'Ow.'

'Don't be so rotten, he's wonderful.'

'I know; he's fucking terrific. I just never imagined him as a cabaret star. This man sticks pins in people.'

'I thought you liked that.'

'You know what I mean.'

Mr Ho permitted two encores and then took his bow, denying all further demands.

'God love the wee man, I could just put him in my pocket and take him home.'

Appearing next to Colin, Mr Ho shook hands politely with Margaret and then gave Colin a huge smile.

The next act was a duo: two elderly gentlemen in evening dress who played the ukelele and the washboard respectively. Both had glistening, crimson faces and swayed where they stood, jogging along neat enough; the washboarder swigging occasionally from an unmarked bottle.

When the ukelelist launched into a tuneless ditty commenting on the character of Jews, Japs, Gerries and Pakkies Colin was the first to grab him by the collar. Graham and Colin huckled off the would-be singer between them while the man with the washboard picked up his instrument and staggered away before Big Douglas could even reach him.

Perfect silence descended slowly as the noise of a gentle scuffle drifted in from outside, then a ragged cheer erupted as Graham, Douglas and Colin reappeared. They were smiling. Margaret felt she should say something to Mr Ho.

'Not at all. They didn't even mention slant-eyed Chinamen, nor our habit of cooking Alsatian dogs and children.'

'I'm sorry anyway.'

'You have nothing to apologise for. This seems to be the general rule: that those not responsible will always apologise for things which are unimportant, not at the heart of the matter. Do you see?'

'Yes.'

'But you feel guilty and so apologise in order to remove your guilt.'

'I suppose.'

'Do you? Or are you allowing me to insult you because I am a member of a racial minority?'

'I think both. You have a lovely singing voice.'

'Thank you, I think so.'

He giggled and squeezed Margaret's hand.

'Now I will present you back to your friend who seems to be slightly wounded although not at all in need of my assistance.'

'What?'

Colin had removed the skin from all the knuckles on his right hand.

'I never hit anyone, only the wall. Big Dougie took care of everything, Graham stood and watched and I punched fuck out one of the walls. It's very dark out there. Oh, Mr Ho, look – '

'Don't mention it, I know, you're sorry and I have an astonishingly wonderful voice. Go with Margaret and have some first aid applied. Some privacy. Go, go.'

So Margaret went off to the back office and fell asleep across three chairs, her head rested in Colin's lap.

That was how Lawrence found them.

'Good evening. Do I know this gentlemen? Do you? I came back to be sure that the evening had passed off well. I returned to thank you for your help. No, don't get up. Why bother now? I thought . . . We'll discuss this on Monday. In private. Because I respect other people's privacy.'

Graham's face appeared in the doorway behind Lawrence.

'How's it going Maggie? You feeling better now? Maggie was taken not well about a half an hour ago, I think it was the heat. That and all the running about she'd been doing. And what an evening, eh? Successful, well behaved and a high point in the life of the community. Provost Grant stuck his head in a while back,

Maggie showed him round. He wanted to wait for you, Mr L. but I think you were elsewhere. Trouble at home was it?'

'No, no trouble thank you.'

Margaret sat up slowly. 'Yes, I'm fine now, thank you, Graham. Ready to start clearing up. Mr Lawrence this is Colin, my fiancé, I think you met earlier. Outside.'

'How do you do, Mr Lawrence?'

'How do I do?' The eyes were dead now, an odd shade of grey clouding across something less pleasant. 'Oh, I'm well, I'm well. I hope Margaret is well, too. Properly taken care of. I hope we're all well. Of course.'

'Oh, we're fine, Mr L. – just fine.' Colin stood as he spoke. There was something a little threatening about the speed with which he moved.

'Well, be seeing you then, Mr L.'

Lawrence stood in the doorway, silent and unblinking as the lights flickered on full in the main room and a final cheer went up.

'Colin and I need to help clear up now, Mr Lawrence.'

'Of course. Of course. I will go home now. I'm glad everything is alright here. Delighted. Goodnight. Goodnight.'

Lawrence quickly, dryly, pecked her cheek and turned away without looking back, his arms folded.

'Goodnight, Margaret.'

She felt she should call something after him, but could think of nothing, no words.

Ashtrays were emptied, tables wiped and the floor mopped down as chairs were stacked by the walls and feet made new tracks of dirt across the wet tiles. Margaret whistled and heard three or four other whistles joining in. Mr Lawrence's car jerked away across the gravel outside.

Graham peeled the last of his notices down. 'Heather, come here and dance, come here till I tell you something.'

He recited, holding the wilting paper up for her to see. ' "But . . . to sing, to dream, to laugh, to go where I please, to stand alone, to be free." To be free, to be free.' He cleared his throat and caught both her hands in his, beginning the Saint Bernard's waltz.

Margaret's last memory of the ceilidh is of dancing a Saint Bernard's waltz with Colin in a room without music, but full of stepping and spinning couples. She can hear the slide and stamp of their feet, steady clapping and someone humming under their breath. And she is sure a familiar mind is watching.

Held in the swing and dance of the carriage, she again has the sensation of being observed and of knowing her observer. She feels something like the small heat of her father's smile and remembers flattening her hands against Colin's back and thinking he danced as if he might be family. It would be good if they could all be together like that.

Going home slow and early in the small hours of Saturday, everybody agreed how well things had gone. Resting through the weekend, sometimes remembering this or that moment; a certain light on a face; everybody was sure of their success. Back at the Factory on Monday, voices were sleepy and contented with now and then a laugh breaking out from nowhere in particular. Everyone, even Bobby The Dug, had made something that worked and was wanted. Cracked it.

Not a smile faded when Mr Lawrence arrived, just before four o'clock. He looked a little tired and he wore a dark suit. Sammy and Lesley and Margaret were all in the front office when he walked in.

'Miss Hamilton.'

He closed the door behind them and spoke to her where they stood, pressing one fist against the wall from time to time, as if he was making a slow punch.

'I'm going to be honest with you, Margaret. I'm going to confide in you. I've done that before and regretted it, but I don't, at the moment, feel that any more harm can be done.

'To begin at the beginning, I returned to this Centre, to the ceilidh, because I wanted to apologise. I wanted to say I was sorry for the incident with my . . . for Daisy. She – well, you saw.

'I also wanted to thank you. I also wanted to speak to you a little, perhaps about nothing very important; it certainly isn't important now. You are easy to talk to. Or I have found you to be. I ask myself why and the answers I find are disturbing. Perhaps you made yourself that way.'

His knuckles touched against the paintwork and Margaret took in a breath.

'No. Don't speak to me just now. *I'm* speaking to *you*. Just listen.

'I came back to see you. For no other reason. To see you. And I find you there, looking up at me with that . . . it was the insolence in your face, not the young man – I could have expected something like that. Your face. To see so clearly in your face what you must have been saying about, laughing about, that fracas in the car-park. Or maybe you were just laughing at me in general. Even pity would have hurt less, or disgust.'

'Mr Lawrence, I never said – '

'It doesn't matter. I'm not interested. It's not important. What counts is that I drove down here to see you and while I was away – perhaps exactly while I was talking to you and your little friend – my wife was sick.'

'I'm sorry.'

'Shut up. She was drunk and lying passed out on her back in our bed. On our bed, actually. And she was sick. She vomited. To be very precise about it, she vomited and then drowned in her vomit. Inhaled it – aspirated – that's a word I hadn't heard until today.

'And really, it's no one's fault. It would have happened sometime, anyway. I can't say she was a very lovable woman, not any more, but, you know, I was quite fond of her in a stupid kind of way. She had very good skin until quite recently; pale, but clear.

'I didn't love her any more. I won't lie. I didn't love her but I wanted her to be alive this morning and she's not. If I hadn't been with you and she hadn't been alone, I believe she would be alive now. Can you see that I . . . don't you feel even a little responsible for this?'

His hand was leaving a red blur now, where it touched the wall.

'Mr Lawrence, I'm very, very sorry. I had no idea. If I . . . is there anything I can do.'

'Do?' He was almost shouting suddenly. 'For whom? Me? Me?'

'Anyone.'

'Oh, just anyone. Well, I suppose that's me. I think you've done enough for me.'

'I wasn't m – '

'Don't say that, I particularly don't want to hear that. Not from you. No, why don't you do something for Daisy. One last good turn.'

'What do you want me to do?'

'What I tell you.'

'Which is?'

'Tell them she's dead. Tell them all that she's dead – all your friends. Have a laugh on me.'

'Mr – '

Sammy stepped into the passage when Lawrence had turned away, almost running from the building; smiling emptily ahead of him and almost running out to his car.

'Sammy, Mr Lawrence, he just . . .'

'We know. We could hear him. We know.'

He looked at Margaret as if there was suddenly something wrong about her face.

'You're being paranoid.'

'What?'

'Paranoid.'

Margaret moved her head from over Colin's shoulder, looked down at him.

'I thought you were asleep.'

His eyes were open now, the streetlight through the window gave them a shine.

'No, I was thinking.'

'That I'm paranoid. The man's wife has died and it's my fault.'

'Of course it's not your fault.'

'I know, I know. No, I don't know, not for sure. I think I should have done something, but, probably it's not my fault. Nobody thinks it is – except for Lawrence. But Lawrence is the only one that matters.'

'Has he done anything? Said something?'

'No. Not really.'

'No threats.'

'No nothing. That's the trouble; he hasn't said or done a thing. He's been polite and so quiet, all the time, quiet.'

'Well, like you say, his wife's just died. It's probably that he's upset.'

'No, no. That's not it. He's thinking. He's thinking. He doesn't know what to do yet so he's not doing anything. He's thinking and then he'll decide. He'll do something.'

'Well, I'm not holding my breath until he does. For Christ's sake. You worry when he's worrying you – you worry when he's not. Every time he makes you like this, he's won.'

'I know, I know.'

They slept that night, uneasily, because they had fitted themselves too close together and what had seemed pleasant at first became hot and constricting. Margaret dreamed something unclear and feverish.

Days ticked by, through and beyond Christmas. On Christmas Day there was no snow and no sign of snow. Margaret and Colin cooked part of a turkey, boiled a pudding, ate until they felt light-headed and then lay on the sofa together feeling domestic. Margaret gave Colin a sweater.

'Very original.'

And Colin gave Margaret a ring.

'This is a ring.'

'Really? Oh, aye, so it is.'

'I mean, this is a ring.'

'Do you know, now I look at it, that's right. See if it fits, I had to guess.'

'I mean – '

'I know what you mean. You can wear it on any finger for any reason. Through your ear, through your nose. Just take it as a present; that's what it is. Don't worry.'

'I'm not worried, but this is important. If you'd told me, I could have come with you. We might have bought it together. We might have talked about it.'

'Don't you like it?'

'Yes, it's lovely. Really. But why didn't we talk.'

'Because I was scared.'

'You were what?'

'Because I was scared. I thought we might have ended up rowing, or something. I mean, it's a ring. That's all. I'd like you to wear it for me. That would be nice. I would like that. If we decided it meant something more than that then, yes, I would like that, too. I would like that very much, Margaret.'

'I did say I'd think about it.'

'But you've said nothing since.'

'Is this an engagement ring?'

'You tell me.'

'No. You tell me if you'd like it to be. Make a decision, go on.'

'I've already made it, for crying out loud.' Colin leaned forward and rested his fists on his knees and she wanted to stroke his neck. He fell back and pulled one palm across his face. 'Alright, alright. This time, right now. Yes, I would like that to be an engagement ring. That was the finger I pictured wearing it. OK?'

'Aye, OK.'

'Mags? Could you say that again, please?'

'OK. This is an engagement ring. Which means we're engaged. Which means we're thinking of being married. How do you feel about that?'

'How do I feel? I'm happy. I'm very happy. You're my darling, you know that, Mags. My darling.'

'That's nice.'

'It's a good thing I don't expect you to be romantic.'

'This has never happened to me before, why should I know what to say? I love you very much, too much, more than I can live with, more than I can live without. I need you more than I can manage. And you're awful nice and I want to marry you. That's all.'

'Oh.'

'But we need to get to know each other a lot for this to work. This is serious stuff. We'll have to get very close. And I'll change. I won't change for you. I'll change because time passes and I'll change for us, or even because of you, but never for you. I won't be someone different for you. I'll wear what I wear and do the things I do. If you marry me, you'll be marrying me, not what you

204

hope I'll turn into. This has to be fair. I'm marrying you for you. Because I like you. I love you. I waited for you.'

'I've never said I wanted you different.'

'I know, I know that. I know you, I think. I'm just trying to be fair. And promise me you'll say when there's something wrong.'

'*If* there's something wrong. It doesn't have to happen.'

'Promise.'

'Promise me the same.'

'I'll try.'

'No.'

'I promise. You.'

'I promise.'

'OK. Do you mind if I say something?'

'Fucksake. Sorry, go on. Say it all.'

'I don't know how to do this. Give me a hug first. No, don't.' She turned her head to one side a touch and then tilted it up, 'Daddy? Daddy, this is Colin. It would be very nice if you liked him, because I do. We would like him to be my husband. I don't know, I don't know if you're there, sometimes I think you are, and, but I'm not sure. I love him; remember I told you that the first time. I think I told you that. Well, it's still there. It's still there. And, Thanks, thank you. Night, night.'

Margaret found Colin was holding her hand very tight. She kissed his knuckles.

'Could you give me a hug now. Then I'll give you the ring back and you can put it on. And I do want to cry. Yes I do want to cry. Yes I do.'

Margaret got used to wearing the ring within weeks, didn't feel it on. Soon a tiny callous formed above it, where it rubbed. Sometimes she would just sit and look at it, not especially thinking of anything. Except perhaps of what Colin thought when he sat and looked at it, too.

She remembered finding her father's wedding-ring in a little box with some collar studs and cufflinks – all things he never wore. She had thought of wearing his ring herself, of having it altered whenever it happened she might need a wedding-ring. Or of turning it into something else. In the end, she took it down to the docks and threw it in the big grey river. She would never have worn it and now no one else could.

Maybe some fisherman would find it in a fish – like the Saint Columba story. She wasn't sure if the river still had fish.

The hardness of her secret ring makes tiny clicks against the window of the train to remind her it's there, she's still wearing it. She thinks how much nicer the journey would be if James was still beside her and feels more than hears the feather-light click, click, click of metal on glass. She remembers the tiny disturbance around her finger from her long drive with Colin.

Three months ago now, they pushed their way out of the city until the road narrowed between dusty, private woods, the trim green of country-club turf, barbed-wire fences around tilting jetties. Their van ground on, its windows open against the heat of a spring sun. Margaret checked Colin's map, unwrapped sweeties for him and pressed them between his soft, warm lips.

But mainly she looked out around her as the hills rose up into mountains and made her ears pop.

'That cottage down there.'

'Where.'

'No, only take a little look, careful.'

'I am being careful, look; both hands on the wheel. What cottage?'

'There's a wee white cottage miles and miles down. I wonder if it's nice there. It looks so fucking nice, I wonder if it could be that good. Or would you get used to it.'

'Lonely, snow in the winter, I don't know. Would you like to live out here?'

'I'd never thought about it. Christ, look at that.'

They slipped down between high, ragged shadows, here and there erased by blanks of snow, then turned into the sun between curves and rushes of fawn, brown, pink, grey, leaf green, shadow green, spring green, black. The road rolled itself along one lochside then twisted and stretched along another while Margaret changed the tape in their machine and rested her hand on Colin's knee, gave a wee squeeze.

They had four days ahead in a caravan at the far end of a little town; four days away from their work, from Lawrence, four days without distractions. Margaret even had Lawrence's blessing before she went. 'Certainly, you have some days in lieu and this would be an opportune moment to take them. Things seem to be rather quiet here. I think we could manage without you. Indeed. Oh, yes indeed.'

At the end of their first day, Margaret could hardly picture where they had been before. She lay in bed, feet still tender from all their walking, still feeling the softness of sheets as something close to pain. When she tried to see the Factory in her head, even Graham's face, his bunnet, she couldn't do it. And then she was surprised by a long, smooth sleep, unbroken. They both woke too hungry to wait and cook their breakfast, piling up cornflakes and spreading their marmalade thick on raw bread.

They picked out hills where the conifers hadn't spread yet, walked on earth and grass that no one was making a matter of signs and wire and ownership. The mornings could be chill, the sky almost white, even a thin rain falling, but then the day would bloom right into the evening, bright and piercing. Their faces and arms coloured quickly and when Margaret washed in the evenings, it seemed she was cleaning off more than dirt. She tingled, felt lighter; as if she was touching Colin through a somehow thinner skin. Colin decided to grow a moustache.

Margaret found they spoke less. She would catch herself taking his hand while they walked. They would stand with their arms laced around each other's backs and she wouldn't know who had started the move that brought them together, hip to hip. It happened that they would touch and touch again, as if they were continuing one movement, or perhaps letting it flow around them like a cloud, a liquid or a light.

Back in the van at the start of another white morning Colin steered them away from the road leading home.

'What are you doing?'

'Getting us lost.'

'You're heading back for that Humph, aren't you. The one in the glen.'

'We've never been up it.'

'I know, I'm not in a rush. It was you who wanted us out by the crack of dawn. It won't take us long to get up the Humph, it's only wee.'

'Is that you insulting my Humph?'

'Not at all, it's a very nice Humph. I've often admired it.'

'We've only been past it twice. Get your hand out of there.'

'Why?'

'Because.'

'Because why?'

'Because if you don't, I'll bite you and I won't stop the car before I do, I'll just steer with my feet. Pervert.'

'I thought you liked it. Especially that.'

'No don't do . . . Oh dear, oh dear. Will you look at that. You did that.'

'No, that's definitely you; I recognise it.'

*

The Humph stood by itself on the table-smooth floor of the glen, something remarkable. Margaret could feel, as she felt in every glen, the bigness of the glacier that must have grown and gouged and ground away what was there. There was a threat, almost too huge to notice, still cold in the air above the sculptured hillsides and the flat, flat plain. The Humph must have been bigger before the glacier came and Margaret and Colin threaded their way towards it as if they were crossing an elemental footprint. An impression of ice.

A white cottage spread its garden just beneath the Humph and an old woman was digging there. Colin nodded his head towards her cardiganed back.

'Do you think if we killed her, we could have her house?'

'Behave.'

Climbing, stone to stone and up through a narrow gateway they found that the shape of the Humph had been added to; unaccidental stones planted beside the ones that the glacier left. Here had used to be a fortress, the heart of a kingdom founded by the same people who had seeded the plain with standing stones and circles, tombs and cairns. The same people carefully topped their dry-stone walls with little upright teeth and shared their graveyard with knights under sculptured slabs. It seemed an odd place.

Colin stood by a curve of stone wall eaten into a bank and took Margaret's hand.

'Whoever they were, they liked their stone.'

'No. They liked butterflies.'

'Oh, aye. Of course.'

'Didn't you notice? All the stones down there, where the sun was shining, they were covered in butterflies.'

'Right. Butterfly worshippers. Very Scottish. Weird all the same. You coming up to the top?'

'I want to put my foot in the footprint first. There, there's one carved out. You see?'

'Aye. My foot was too big.'

'That doesn't surprise me.'

Another eight steps, maybe ten, and they conquered the Humph. Suddenly.

'Jesus fuck.'

'My God, Jesus God. Just fuck.'

The floor of the plain birled back to the edge of the glen, hills strangely diminished. The earth fell away all about them and they seemed to have stumbled up to the heart of the world. They laughed. They turned and turned and laughed.

'We can't be up this high. I mean this is a Humph, not a fucking mountain.'

'I don't care. Colin McCoag, this is some Humph.'

'Some Humph, some Humph.'

Margaret was still sitting on the Humph's brow, looking out and holding Colin, when a jogger pounded and scuttered his way by them. He circled and plunged down the way he had come without a pause. Colin squeezed her waist then tickled just a little.

'Silly bugger.'

'Well, it's not the way I'd do it, I know. He'll never know he's been here.'

'So what would you do up here?'

'We won't be doing anything up here, Elder McCoag.'

'Spoilsport.'

'It's not exactly private.'

'You could kiss me though, couldn't you?'

'Yes, I could.'

His tongue flickered around hers and brushed her lips, as if it was laughing. She smiled in return and smoothed her hand round and over to hold the fine skin at the back of his neck, to push her fingers into his hair. Colin's hand fluttered over her nipple, brushing through her blouse, their hands held each other, laced and unlaced fingers, gripped around backs. Colin's palms and forehead tasted salt, his hair smelled of sun, musty gorse and sun.

Margaret found herself pulling Colin by the hair, drawing his face away so that she could see it, then taking his head in her hands.

'Oh, God. I do love you. Colin, you're beautiful. You are beautiful. I want to take you home with me. I want to eat you up. All of you. Darling. I do love you.'

'Eat me up then. Eat me up.'

Colin's van was already an hour nearer home when Margaret shook her head and laughed.

'What is it?'

'I've just noticed, we're neither of us wearing our seat-belts. A couple of days in the country and we go to pieces.'

'It's called being relaxed; some people do it all the time.'

'Mm. I know. It was lovely up there. Thanks for suggesting it.'

'Are we talking about the Humph or the holiday?'

'Both. I mean it, thanks.'

'You don't have to thank me. I wouldn't have gone without you, wouldn't have thought of it. And it's been lovely to see you so happy. So calm. You were almost like another person.'

'Thanks a lot.'

'You know what I mean. You were more like yourself than I've seen you for ages. It was lovely.'

'Well, it was good. It was nice. And you've been good to be with, too.'

'Margaret, can I ask you something.'

'Sure.'

'It's just, that job's so fucking bad for you. It's so pointless. Why don't you give it up. We could live off my wages.'

'I see.'

'Until you got something else. I could help you out until we found something better. And when we're married, there might be other things. Just think, you wouldn't have to plod about in jeans and sweaters all the week.'

'I didn't realise my job was pointless.'

'I mean it's a waste of what you could be doing.'

'Whereas sitting at home and living off your money wouldn't be. Because I'd be so much better dressed.'

'You just, I wish you could see the change there's been in you, only in these few days.'

'Yes, I remember. You said I seemed like another person. That seemed to be your ideal. I've been on holiday, Colin, that's always nice. It has nothing to do with real life. What are you telling me. I have to stay on holiday now, for ever.'

'Oh for fuck's sake.'

'My own thoughts entirely. Of course, the great thing about being up here was that you could get your hole whenever you liked. Let's not forget that. Available day and night – ideal.'

'You weren't complaining.'

'I never fucking do, do I.'

'What?'

'Nothing.'

'No, what did you mean? I try to give you some advice which, fuck knows, you need and suddenly you've only been putting up with me all this time. It's entirely unreasonable for me to want you to listen to what I'm fucking telling you. Your idea of a marriage is you do what you fucking like.'

'You'd rather I just did what I was told. I happen to think that selling pensioners satellite TV should be illegal. Do I ever say you should give up your job? At least I'm trying to help folk.'

'How can you help folk when you canny even help yourself. It's pathetic.'

'Shut up, Colin, just shut up. Before I do something I'm sorry for. Just take us fucking home.'

'I'll take us where I fucking want. I trusted you. I fucking trusted you. Fucking pathetic.'

Margaret reached to snap on the radio, then folded her arms and sat while its voices smothered their silence. She pressed one elbow down on her stomach, where a tension was starting to build, a chill. The van passed a car with its bonnet crushed, its roof cut neatly off. Firemen and policemen still walked round it., stepping silently through a sheen of broken glass. A little white cloth had been folded over the back of the driver's seat. Its brightness framed a large stain of blood, unsubtle in the flat afternoon sun. Margaret found she had too much saliva in her mouth, started choking it quietly down.

Colin whispered, 'Jesus,' but when Margaret turned to face him he said nothing more, apparently intent on the road ahead. As they moved into the city, the radio described their accident, told them who died, gave it reality.

'The Underground isn't far from here.'

Colin dawdled the van towards the kerb.

'Is the back door locked?'

'Here's the keys.'

'OK. I'll get my bag, then. Thank you.'

Margaret walked slowly to stand by the passenger door. Stooping down to pass through the keys, she paused for a while, simply watching Colin's face. He seemed upset, less angry and more liable to cry. She knew she didn't want him to be upset. She knew she didn't want him to drive away. She knew she didn't want to apologise.

'That's my bag fetched. I've just thought, I've no money left. I don't even have my fare for the underground.'

'Uh huh.'

It seemed important for her to slide herself back inside the van, to tug her holdall on to her lap and close the door.

'What are you doing?'

'Could you give me a lift back home. It's on your way. Please.'

'Fine, fine, fine. Just put on your seat-belt, will you?'

'I'll do that.'

By the time they reached her street, Margaret felt almost light-headed. Her stomach was throbbing in time with her pulse. She gave a start when Colin spoke.

'This is you.'

'I know. Colin, I want to touch you.' The noise of motors ran through the pause. 'Did you hear me? I want to – '

'I heard.'

'Would you, do you want that?'

'Of course I fucking want that. I want you. I don't know how to get you.'

'I'm here now.'

'I don't know.'

'We have to get to know each other. We have to get used to each other.'

'I can't even reach you now, your fucking duffle-bag's in the way. Always something.'

'I'll put it outside. I can hold your hand now. Feel.'

Margaret took Colin's left hand in her right and he let the engine die. She could feel his blood beating in his veins, a squeeze against her palm, a rearrangement of fingers.

'Colin, I want us to be together. So much. It can't be this hard. This makes no sense. Oh.'

He was crying, without sound, his mouth very slightly open.

'Baby, don't cry because of me. Please don't. Come in, come up with me.'

'No.'

'Come up. I want you to.'

'No. I can't now. I don't know what I'm doing.'

'Well, I'll call you in a couple of hours. Will I call you?'

'Alright. Yes, do that. Maggie, Maggie, I don't know.'

'I'll call you and we'll talk. We can go for a drive. Will you be alright? You shouldn't be driving, you know.'

'I'm alright.'

She lifted his hand and kissed it, then got out of the van. Once she'd closed the door, she tapped on the window till he rolled it down.

'I will ring you and you must take care. Go and have a bath, have something to eat.'

She waved as the van pulled away, the sound of her tapping on the window still in the air. Click, click, click. Her ring had made a good noise on the glass. A useful noise. Click, click, click.

It was an all-night place, slightly grubby, with high, plate-glass windows that let in the dark. Margaret had already drunk one coffee when Colin arrived. He turned in the doorway, smiled when he picked out her face, then seemed to remember something which took his smile away and left him tired.

When he came back from the counter, he put his coffee cup down next to Margaret's, but didn't sit. He stood behind her, resting his hands on her shoulders, leaning down to smell her hair and kneading her jacket in his hands.

'What's the matter? Come and sit down.'

'I will, I will.'

And he slowly moved to take the chair opposite. Margaret had the impression that he'd already told her goodbye: that whatever they said could not alter what he had decided. He had driven away and not come back. The hours had passed in a different day and they were not together now. It could not be possible for them to be so together and then so apart inside the same day.

She watched her face in the blackness of the window, her nose illuminated, the rest in shade, and heard Colin start to speak. It seemed she had heard him say these things before, it seemed they were less real than they should be.

'I can't do this any longer. It isn't working. I've never felt more uncomfortable or unhappy in my life. Never.'

He did look unhappy.

'We don't deserve this. I mean, I'm fucking sure I don't. I'm sorry. I've thought about it all night. Longer than that, on and off, but for the whole of tonight. There really isn't a way out. Either we live together, we both commit ourselves, the whole thing, or we call it a day; we don't see each other. Not at all. I am sorry.'

Once Colin has left her, Margaret will twist her ring around her finger without knowing it and she will say nothing and let him go out of sight along the street. She will tell his name to a stranger, then buy herself her third cup of coffee and start to drink. Slowly.

She was already feeling almost better and somehow expecting that Colin would walk back in and feel much better, too. Some kind of argument broke out behind her; two female voices, young and quickly screaming. Two waitresses and a man in a suit rushed between tables and then moved towards Margaret, pushed back towards the door by two girls.

'There's nothing in my fucking bag – that's all! And would you mind not breaking my fucking stuff. Ian!'

A thin, pale man was waiting in the street. He walked away.
'Ian!'

The staff linked arms to bar the door, slid bolts and talked about policemen coming. The girls screamed and battered, then subsided, the one with the blonde hair now crying and swaying.

'I'm only sixteen.'

No one in the café moved, or looked up. Margaret heard cars pass outside, one girl crying, another breathing, both pale with serious eyes.

And then the remarkable thing happened. Margaret saw the

darker girl wander, pause, drift quite close to her table and then walk through the plate-glass window. Simply walk, head tilted forward. Away.

The crash was almost liquid, huge, and there were screams as a tide of glass washed back and into the café. A piece landed near Margaret's hand, but she did not move, even flinch, because she was watching the girl disappear at a run and wondering if there was anything now she would walk through a window for. She didn't know what would make her do that, what would be strong enough.

There was only a little blood dotted over the floor. The only real sign that anything had taken place, blood in droplets and a hole leading through a window into the night.

If this had happened in any other week.

Margaret often thought that. 'If this had happened in any other week.'

She is phoning a friend in London now. Margaret's friend is a woman called Helen. They were at university together and have seen each other only once since then. They have also sent letters, from time to time.

One hand holds the receiver, while the other dials and Margaret thinks, 'If this had happened in any other week.'

Making an unknown phone ring, miles and miles away, Margaret imagines a face which no longer exists, because it is seven, or five, or three years out of date and because parts of it have simply been forgotten. The voice is much the same.

'Maggie? Fuck! That's very crazy. Maggie!'

'That's my name, don't wear it out.'

'What, Mags?'

'Nothing. Yes, hello. How are you?'

'Me? Great. But listen, I've just done your Tarot reading – it's on the floor, right now. What? Oh, sorry Mags, we've shuffled you up and now it's someone else. Someone you don't know. In fact I don't know him, either. Hey, could we get a bit of quiet here, this is a person calling from Scotland? Sorry, Maggie. But really, it was very odd. You been suicidal recently? If you don't mind me asking. The nine of swords came up, but only as a past influence. God, it's good to hear from you. Are you coming down?'

'Well, yes, I am. Just for a while. But it might be permanent in the end.'

'Well, no problem. Do stay here. It's a much nicer flat than the last one. We do things together.'

'Like Tarot readings.'

'That's the latest, yes. I think we've done everyone possible now. Fictional characters next. When are you coming?'

'The end of the week. If that's OK.'

'Any time. Give me a ring and we'll sort out how you get here. I'm rehearsing another one of these profit-share things, so I'm out in the day. Fuck, this'll be good. What? Oh, Paul's just asked if you've got nice legs. You'll be glad to know that he's not really a sexist bumhole and he also doesn't live here. It just feels like it.'

'It doesn't sound as if things have changed much.'

'No, well, they don't do they? How's things with thing, with Colin? Not hot?'

'Not really.'

'All in the cards, my dear, all in the cards. You can tell me when you come down. Don't worry, you're going to get very spiritual and a good and trusty friend is going to gallop up and help you out.'

'Did it say anything about getting a job?'

'Oh. Serious shit. What have you been doing? No don't tell me now, it'll cost too much.'

'Yes. And I'll have to go now. But I'll ring you again. And thanks for letting me stay.'

'No problem. I'll come up and stay with you, too. See the Year of Culture and all that. Really, no problem. It'll be nice to see you.'

'Good, well, that's me away then.'

'Bye, bye.'

'Hey, Helen.'

'Hm? Yes? Sorry, did you say something?'

'No, no, I ran out of steam. Just, just, thanks. I'm glad you were in.'

'Look, do you need to talk? I can ring you back.'

'No. I'm fine. It'll be great to see you again. Bye, Helen. Bye.'

Margaret doesn't replace the receiver right away, she listens to the click of disconnection and the dull hum that follows it. She feels lonely enough to cry.

Now, she rings Colin's number again. Again he doesn't answer. This is because he isn't home, but the lack of reply feels more personal than that.

And he should be in. Since Monday morning, she has rung him at times when he should have been in and he hasn't answered. There is something wrong. Since he left the café on his own, of course, there's been something wrong, because they are apart now, but this is something different. This feels like something different. If it had only happened in any other week. This week, there is too much going on.

She should have known on Monday. Even Monday was bad. The night before, she had slept well enough; one day into not having Colin. She felt quite light, relieved. It couldn't be possible things were really over and when they had got back together, they could start from fresh again. There were mistakes that needn't be repeated. Perhaps it would even be peaceful if she was alone for a while. Margaret was in the mood for peace. But Monday hadn't been peaceful.

She arrived nice and early, ready to fit back into the Factory, knowing there was typing to be done, a few things to clear up.

'No, that's alright, we did that, Maggie.' Lesley smiled and pushed a mug of coffee towards Margaret. 'Things are really very quiet, just now, you wouldn't believe.'

'Oh, well, I'll do the stocktake for the café, then.'

'No need, put your feet up. Take it easy. Oh, and good news – Lawrence won't be in today, he told us, so why bother running about when there's nothing to do? How's Colin? Did you have a nice time?'

'Yeah, fine. I think I'll get a biscuit, then, if there's nothing else to do.'

For the first time, Margaret began to feel how much she would miss Colin; that it was quite unlikely she would be seeing him again.

The day passed in a blur; Lesley chatting, even joking, the Factory oddly quiet. Graham wasn't there and Margaret would have liked to talk to him.

A letter was waiting when Margaret got home. Not from Colin.

Dear Miss Hamilton,

It has been drawn to my attention that your general conduct has failed on several occasions to meet management guidelines and terms specifically agreed in your contract of employment.

In the light of this and two specific instances of serious misconduct, I regret to inform you that the Community Link Centre management can no longer retain your services as Centre Assistant. Kindly accept this as one month's notice of dismissal, as dated above.

It was from Lawrence, of course. And it should have arrived in any other week but this one. Not now. She wasn't concentrating.

An appointment had been made for her to see Lawrence the following morning. She managed to be less than early and walked straight to Lawrence's office, speaking to no one. She knew that the letter had been typed on the office word-processor, she knew there had been no 'serious misconduct' and she knew that she was angry. She was angry enough for it to show. Even Lawrence flinched a little when he saw her.

'I believe my letter made an arrangement for ten o'clock.'

'That's right.'

'I don't suppose there's any reason for your being twenty minutes late?'

'No, there isn't.'

'I see. We'll get straight to business, then, allow me to explain. Lesley McGavin has all the necessary papers with her in the office and there is, in fact, no reason for me to see you. I just wanted to see your face. Do you understand that?'

'I do not. And I don't understand why I'm being fired.'

'I think I made that clear.'

'No, you made nothing clear. I could guess at a reason, of course, but your letter said misconduct – what misconduct? I haven't done anything.'

'I was hoping we might leave just a little of this unsaid. So much of it, after all, has always been unspoken. Your choice. Your technique. Until you'd finished the job. But we can always go through this piece by piece, just to please you.'

'Mr Lawrence, I don't know what you mean. Again.'

'Of course you don't. Of course. That's always the case, isn't it, with sexual harassment. Flirtation. Teasing. Matters of that kind. People always talk about misunderstandings. Women talk about misunderstandings. You're telling me you want words. You and your friend, Graham, you like words, don't you.'

'What exactly are you implying, Mr Lawrence.'

'Not implying. Saying. I'm saying you made a fool of me. Socially, professionally, personally, sexually. Very thorough. And when you were finished, I was supposed to creep away out of sight. That it? The shamefaced, dirty old man.'

'How would you describe yourself.'

'Well, I'd love to argue the point with you, but the fact is, I don't have to. I don't even have to see you, not ever again. You may be interested to know that I will find myself unable to give you much by way of a reference. To that, I can add that any difficulty, any awkwardness you might consider generating would prove highly unfortunate for you. I am tired of dealing with difficulties that you have caused. So . . .'

Lawrence lifted a paper from his desk, a single, typed sheet; dated and signed.

'This is a letter, unsolicited of course, which testifies that on two separate occasions you supplied a member of the Youth Theatre with cannabis – rather banal these days, but still illegal. You don't have anything to say?'

'What can I say? This is nonsense. Nobody would believe this, nobody.'

'I believe it – I always believe what I see in writing. Most people do. Of course, no one need know about this, if you go peacefully, like a good wee girl. You won the battle, I won the war.'

'Who wrote the letter?'

'You don't want to know.'

'It can't have been anyone in the Youth Theatre.'

'Because they all love you so much. You know what that is, Miss Hamilton? Arrogance. I may not be a popular man, one of the boys, likeable, but at least I never assume that I'm loved. I never take love for granted.'

'I am very sorry about your wife.'

'Oh, shut up. "I am very sorry." You're pathetic. Unconvincing. You'd like to know who wrote this letter? It was Raymond. Raymond Turner.'

'Raymond? I don't know any – Oh. Gus. You mean Gus.'

'I mean Raymond Turner, a young man who understands how things work. By August the Community Link Centre will be closed; the end. And in the spring we reopen; new funding, new premises and a new clientele. We'll provide a better service on better terms; something professional. We'll be working with people who want quality and who'll work for it. You could have been there, too, but not now, of course. Our new centre will teach and train, be responsible, support local business, and for everything it does, it will be paid.

'I know you'll find that hard to understand. I know you'll find it even harder not to tell anybody about our wicked plans. But then you'll remember this letter and you'll be sensible. Or, as you might put it, you'll sell out to save your own skin. Just like Raymond. He needed a job – he'll get one. I was glad to help him out. Bright boy.'

'Mr Lawrence, all of this has nothing to do with me. Not even your slimy, wee fantasies have anything to do with me. I hope your new Centre does well. For the sake of some people here who are my friends. And, more than anything, I hope that none of the women who work for you will ever have to come in contact with that thing you call your mind.'

'Is that all?'

'That's all.'

'I take it we'll agree to differ, then.'

'And I'll go quietly, yes. What's the point in anything else. Pardon me if I don't shake your hand. Oh, and Mr Lawrence.'

'Yes?'

'Take a running fuck to yourself. Good morning.'

Margaret went to sit in the café and watched the television. She thought of several other things she could have said. Too late now.

She knew what she would have told Colin about it; what he would have said. At one time, she had told her father everything that happened to her. She had taken it all home to him and made it entirely real, sometimes for the first time. And now, for the first time, Margaret realised she had begun to do the same with Colin. Without him, she had less reality.

Perhaps he would be in if she called him now. Perhaps she should try.

Behind her, Margaret knew, Lesley would be peering through the office window, ready with whatever papers she'd been given to dole out. Ready to say that she and Sam had known nothing about it at all. Fuck her, she could wait.

Everybody could wait. She was going outside to find a payphone, get some privacy. Some fucking week.

In Colin's flat, the phone rang out, stopped and rang again for a long, long time. Nobody answered, nothing moved. Behind the door, there were three envelopes, two in brown and one in white. There was a partly unpacked bag on the kitchen floor and dust was beginning to gather. Everywhere, dust.

Colin hasn't been home since Saturday. His phone has disturbed itself and letters have arrived, but no message has reached him.

'Colin McCoag.'

'What?'

Heading away from the café and from Margaret, careless of where he was walking, Colin found himself surprised.

'Colin McCoag?'

'What?'

He hadn't been concentrating. Two men stepped up and beside him, as if they were part of some dance, as if all they ever did was to move in tight beside strangers and not let them go.

'He is Colin McCoag, though, isn't he?'

'Aye, I know his face. He's just a shy boy.'

The cab turned and stopped as though someone had hailed it, waited until Colin was inside, then jerked away. The voices round him made no sense, they came at him through music, nice music he recognised. A face was almost familiar as the streetlights rolled across it. He pulled away from the hands that held him.

'Oh, now he's waking up.'

'Silly cunt. Does he no know that door willnae open – no while we're moving.'

'And we can lock them when we're still. A great thing, your black hack. Keep him away fae that window, but. We don't want to lose him like that.'

Odd thoughts came into Colin's head. He was punched a little, but mainly kicked, really just stamped on, by the end. He wanted to say who he was, to find out why this was happening. He wanted to see these people's faces and explain that he was fit, very strong and healthy and they could only be doing this to him because they had done it before. They were used to it. He realised it wasn't safe, not safe enough, just to be fit.

He was sure he was shouting something, felt his face rip down against the window, then the door, then down to the floor again, and was almost certain that somebody out on the pavement had waved and laughed at him.

'Shut up, wullye?'

'Fuckin desperate, eh?'

'Too fuckin right.'

Colin listened to the niceness of the music. It was so nice now that it made him want to cry. The floor swung underneath him, lights stretched and sank away and he knew he would be sick soon and he knew he didn't want to need false teeth. They were going to ruin his mouth, that was obvious.

At about the time that Margaret was slowly walking home, without minding the dark, Colin was lying under a sheen of music, moving east and away from her. He would sometimes catch the height of a floodlit building as his head rocked round, seeing perhaps a descending perspective of arches and blank, black glass, finally knowing the sounds he heard were Mozart, something by Mozart, something sad. So sad.

'Mr McCoag? Colin? Wake up. Was he really so very trouble-some? How can I make him understand me when he's like this? You don't think ahead.'

'We did our best, sir. He wouldn't settle down and there were folk about.'

'You know what like the town is on Saturday night, sir. Revellers. Everywhere.'

Colin lay on his back with his eyes closed as voices circled round him, echoed a little with the sound of shoes on a bare wood floor. It was quite cold.

'Will we put the tape on now, sir?'

'Yes.'

'Which would you prefer, sir?'

'I felt in the mood for the *Prague*.'

'We do have that, sir; we have K 504.'

'But you've been playing him the Clarinet Concerto. If I change now, then there's hardly any point in bothering. Ah!'

Colin flinched and felt the deeper of the voices pad up close. Smile.

'He is awake. I thought he was. The Clarinet Concerto now. Thank you.'

The niceness came back in the air and Colin opened his eyes. They blinked and blurred, focused enough to show him a huge, dark room with three men in it. A new face, another one he almost knew. Or was he in a condition to almost know everyone? He felt he might be.

'No, don't try to move. If you do, the gentlemen who brought you here will stop you. Will kick seven shades of shite right out of you. Why? Well, we have our reasons.'

Colin made a noise, felt a noise in his mouth.

'Alright, I'll tell you, although I would rather listen to Mozart than hear myself speak. You were a cheeky boy. Isn't that right?'

'Very fucking cheeky.'

'You upset a little business I was planning, insulted one of my employees. In a public place. Oh, but you did, don't shake your head, it will only annoy me. We were trying to offer a service to the community, loans for anyone who needs them, any time. You stopped us providing that service. You said bad things. So I think you should apologise. Mr Smith, over there, he's the man you insulted. On you go. Don't worry that you can't walk. I think he'd actually prefer you to be crawling.'

'Oh, that's right, sir.'

The Adagio rippled over the boards and through the dust Colin lifted as he moved. He kissed feet as he was told to, fat notes cool inside his head, running up and up, most especially sweetly, even when feet kicked his face, his kidneys, and set him off crawling again to somewhere else.

'Mr Smith and Mr Smith, I think you have been telling little lies. Mr McCoag is no trouble at all. He only cries too much which hurts nobody but himself. No, leave him lie.'

Colin felt himself abandoned, sank one cheek to the boards without feeling when it touched, slightly aware that a ragged edge of tooth was tearing something.

'You are an example, Colin. People will hear about you and will not admire what you did. They will not wish to repeat it. This is our own small Terror, Colin. You can gather it every day from everywhere; post offices and court rooms, your evening paper, your evening streets. We just make our own use of it. This is the way we live, do you see; we cannot exist outside society and so we do our best to use it. To offer it reflections of itself. But because this is so wasteful, so negative, I like to bring something in with a little heart. I like to give. Don't I?'

'Generosity itself, sir.'

'I play you Mozart. Because you will never forget tonight, you'll dream about it in every detail, sharp and fine. So you will never forget this Mozart. You will be a man who dreams the Clarinet Concerto, you will have it all there, tight inside your head. What I wouldn't give for that. I have made you an example but now you can learn, you can enrich your life.'

'I don't think I'll ever listen to Mozart again.'

It became dark very soon after that.

'Mr McCoag, I know you're awake. You are nursing resentments against us. Very natural, I'm sure, but very destructive. For you. Bad for the soul and we want you to have such a very healthy soul. Now we are going to drive them out. Deal with his mouth.'

Colin's mouth was filled with something, filled and over-filled until the floor twisted up underneath him and his arms and legs stretched endlessly away in the most curious pain.

Quite quickly, he discovered the pain was in his hands and

then his feet. Enormous. They must be cutting off his hands and feet. How could they do that? He would die.

Again, the clarinet was playing, singing, humming, turning his brain in its hands and carrying words.

much worse

dirty nails

appreciate the effort

shoes

Mr Smith

fine

stig

YOU'LL HAVE

STIG

concentrate   don't   go   away   from   us
STIGMATA

JUST LIKE BABY JESUS

COLIN

colin

COLIN

COLIN

COLIN

COLIN

COLIN

COLIN

COLIN

colin

co

CHRIST

LOOK AT THAT.

He couldn't remember them leaving, only that he was aware,
sometimes, of being alone and afraid of rats. He also had a great
fear of turning in his sleep.

Once he dreamed he was falling and cried out, tried to reach,
to reach something.

Colin woke in the chill, misty morning left by a clear, clear night
with the man who was called Mr Webster kneeling on his arms.
This prevented Colin moving and pulling at the nails they had
fixed through his hands and feet and was a charitable, almost
loving act.

Colin found himself unable to speak, but listened to Mr Webster speaking with such a focus of attention that he would later remember everything, even the spaces where Mr Webster took his breath. There was a strangely musical quality to his voice. Music from a bright mouth.

'Good morning. I like you.'

It slowly became clear that the night was really over and this was the morning come and no one had died, although some things were different. Colin was very cold, shivering in a way he had no power to stop, glad of the warmth from Webster's breath, the touch of his hands. There was something very solid against his feet. Perhaps a wall.

'I believe we must learn from everything. I believe that nothing ever happens by accident.'

Colin became slowly aware that he had pissed himself, but couldn't remember when. He felt ashamed when Webster looked at him.

Even when the ambulance came, following hard behind its lovely and unmistakable sirens, Colin was still listening to Webster, playing him over and over again inside his head.

'Do every tiny thing you want to do.'

Those words.

'We might have to do it all again: waste everyone's time. Be alive, Colin, don't forget.'

Policemen arrived, blanched and moved away from where Colin lay, and then there were soft hands all around and soft voices. Everything was soft – even Webster, Webster's voice repeating, 'This was a good lesson, Colin, don't forget it.'

Colin fainted when he saw the pliers. Never felt the pain.

One morning, Margaret receives a letter from Mr Ho which tells her just a little about Colin. About what happened. Mr Ho writes very carefully. He says Colin is safe in hospital now, beginning his recovery.

Mr Ho leaves Margaret his office telephone number and says he will take her to Colin on the evening of whichever day she calls. He does not say if Colin has asked her to come. His letter arrives in the first post on Wednesday and that evening, Margaret goes to the hospital.

They drove into the car-park in Mr Ho's burgundy Rover, then walked into the heat and light and tension of the hospital.

'You should sit down, now.'

'What?'

'We will sit here, by the flower shop and gather our thoughts. Something unpleasant has happened to Colin and you have been very good, for whatever reason, in not asking about exactly what. I would like to say that you shouldn't worry. This will all seem very trite, I know, but I will say it anyway – only his body is sick. Everything else is quite well, so he will get better. He may even get better than he was.'

'Does he know I'm coming?'

'I'm not sure.'

'We split up.'

'I know he would like to see you. He has almost no family, you understand? Up until now, only I have been to see him. There are nicer things for him to look at than a rotund acupuncturist. But, if you don't mind, I will go in and see him first.'

Mr Ho stood up neatly, scooping up one of her hands between his smooth palms.

'Will you come with me? Now? We have to take the lift.'

Margaret could feel herself starting to cry. Mr Ho would only have to do one more considerate thing, only look after her a little bit more and she would let go entirely, she would weep. She cleared her throat, bending forward, still sitting.

'Is he in pain?'

'He has been. His . . . you'll see. Everything's going to be fine.'

At any time, Margaret can recall how Colin looked that evening. A creature, a wounded something, a figure laid out on its tomb.

The coverlet over his bed was lemon yellow, the sheets and pillows white like his bandages. She found herself looking at the bandages round his hands, the soft, white bundles his hands had become. She had thought she would hold his hands. She had wanted to.

'Colin. Are you awake?'

He had a cage over his feet.

'Colin. I didn't know. Mr Ho, he – '

Although Colin never wore pyjamas, he was dressed in a pyjama jacket now. She didn't know how he could stand it – the heat and the sheets and the jacket. How did they get his hand bundles through the sleeves?

When his eyes opened, she had to look at them. And his face.

'Hiya. Don't speak if it hurts too much. Oh, I didn't know where you were. Baby. You worried me.'

Colin flinched when she lifted her hand to his head and she felt herself start to sweat. Her stomach flickered and her skin tightened down along her back.

'It's alright. I won't hurt you. I won't hurt you. Just touch your hair, I'm just touching your hair.'

For most of her visit, she sat where he could see her, with one hand reached to touch his head. Colin never spoke, only looked at her.

Even now, on her train, Margaret closes her eyes to imagine Colin in his yellow hospital bed. Even now, it is better to close her eyes because she will probably cry. Outside the ward, that first evening, she cried. Mr Ho held her and rubbed her back while she cried. When she had finished, he held her hands and smiled at her and made her cry again.

It is difficult being here, in this carriage, tugged further and further south when Colin is still at home, still getting used to walking and feeding himself, still giving just a little start whenever the wind shakes the windows, whenever the doorbell rings.

She misses him. She misses her daddy and she misses Colin more.

The walls by the side of the track are very strange now, grey brick and black brick and honey brick. Margaret has entered a foreign country. She remembers seeing waxwings searching the grass when she was at university and suddenly feeling homesick because they were not Scottish birds. There was something a little impossible about them. And that was all it took to make you miss things, a mild impossibility, a slight difference of birds.

Margaret stares out at trees of an alien green and reminds herself that her ticket is a return. There are trains up and down from Scotland every day and she does have that return. An open return. She closes her eyes again. Someone has left the carriage for a smoke, she can smell its thin sourness drifting in.

Margaret knew she couldn't face the Factory again before she even left the hospital. Mr Ho patted her arm.

'I will telephone them in the morning. Some people would rather work through pain, some people would rather not – particularly when their employers are bastards.'

'Yeah, well.'

'I'll call and say you will probably be there on Monday, but then again, you might not. Do you think you'll sleep tonight?'

'I think so. I don't know why, but I feel very tired. I'll sleep.'

'Good. You and Colin, you both should sleep. But this is my number at home. If you would like to phone me during the night, I will be glad to speak to you. It would be a pleasure, in fact. Now. Down to the car.'

Margaret folded the piece of paper into her pocket as she walked, thinking of how long it would take before Colin could fold anything, hold anything.

On Friday morning, Lesley phoned. It took Margaret a while to recognise the voice. She sat up in bed and tried to get her mind to focus.

'Hello, Maggie, that is Maggie?'

'Yes?'

'This is Lesley. You know, from work. Look, I'm. This is all very difficult for us.'

'It isn't too wonderful for me.'

'I'm ever so sorry about Colin. It was in the paper. It sounded, well, it sounded – '

'If you're really interested, I can tell you how it looked.'

'I know you're upset.'

'Good. So now we both know.'

'And I've got a message from Mr Lawrence. He's decided to give you compassionate leave.'

'I'm honoured.'

'You'll still get paid and everything, but you just won't need to come back.'

'What?'

'Well, obviously you'll need to come in for your things and all that, but – He says you needn't come back to work. You can stay off until your notice runs out.'

'Why?'

'I don't know. Who ever does with him. Look, we really will. We'll miss you. You'll be missed. The kids have been asking for you. And Graham.'

'Which kids?'

'Oh, all of them: Elaine, Susan, Tam, Gus.'

'Gus? Gus was asking for me?'

'Yes, why?'

'No reason. Well, thanks for the call.'

'There's no need to be like this, you know. We're all doing our best under very difficult circumstances. I've heard rumours about our funding.'

'Really? That's awful. I'm just worrying about a man who's in hospital because he's been crucified and now he can't walk, or do up a button, or wipe his own arse. You should come and look at his face, Lesley – it's green. There are the cuts and bruises and the swelling, but basically his face is green. It didn't used to be that colour. And all I can do is sit here and hope he'll get better and know that he'll be off work for months and know that I'll be out of a job in three weeks' time. Would you like to tell me how we're going to live? No, of course not, you've got so much on your mind.'

'There's really no talking to you, is there? No wonder Lawrence wants you out the way. You never knew when you were well off, that's your trouble.'

'Well, I don't mean to add to your worries, but it's not just me that's going out the way. You and Sammy are next. It's all change down the Factory. Everybody out. And keep hold of your knickers. As far as Lawrence is concerned, you'll be next.'

'I don't know what you're talking about.'

'I know.'

Margaret hung up the phone. Then she picked it up and threw it against the wall. Then she picked up the alarm clock and threw that, too. The telephone survived, but the alarm didn't. Its glass had shattered. The alarm clock her father had bought her, she couldn't think how long before: its glass was shattered and the hinge on the case was bent.

Colin was frightening for Margaret when she took delivery of him.

'I don't think they should have let you out. They said they couldn't spare your bed any longer. Can you believe that – you can only be ill for as long as we don't need the bed.'

'You can phone and ask if they'll take me back.'

'I would rather have you here where I can see you, I just don't know if I'm doing the right things. What happens if – I mean, how could they ever be sure of where you were going, if you'd be alright?'

'They weren't sure. I wasn't. What do you mean, what happens if – what happens when I get worse? Why don't you just send me back to my own place. This isn't fair, you don't want me here. We decided that before. Before this happened.'

'Colin, I know you're annoyed that you can't do things, I know this is not ideal, I know it hurts. But we're doing our best. Me and you and Mr Ho, we're doing well.'

'When are you going away?'

'Away?'

'I heard you on the phone last night. It's all I can do now;

listen. You were talking to Helen. She's in London. Are you going to London?'

'I was thinking about it. I called her to say it was off. I'm not going anywhere.'

'You should go. You'd get a job down there. Go.'

'I don't want to go just now. I would rather be here. We can both go down later, try it down there. I would rather – oh, fuck you're impossible.'

'Aye, go on, walk out on me. You know I can't follow you. You could be doing anything through there, you could be fucking. I couldn't do a thing about it.'

'What did you say?'

'Oh, the nurse is back. I must have really upset her, to get her to stay in the same room with me, oh fucking dear. I said, you could be fucking through there – I wouldn't know. I couldn't stop you.'

'And who would I be fucking?'

'How would I know?'

'I don't know – you're the expert. You tell me. Who would I fuck? Who have I ever fucked?'

'The German student.'

'One night. After you left me. Who else?'

'How would I know?'

'Because I told you. Because I told you everything. No one else but you. There's no one else that made me feel like this.'

'Except for the German student.'

'I was drunk. Have I ever said I didn't want you?'

'Of course not. You didn't have to. It was fucking obvious.'

It was hard not to just argue with him when he wanted an argument. She didn't want to score points any more, to tally up the battles and the wars. Probably only the smell of pain around him was stopping her from telling him to get to fuck.

And Colin looked different now. There was something about him, under the paleness and the scars. A piece had been added or removed and he seemed somehow much closer to her than he had been. She could feel him close, all over the house – in rooms he hadn't visited since he arrived. Or maybe she was closer to him, she wasn't sure who'd moved.

'I've never said I didn't want you and it has never been true. I've always wanted you. Sometimes I need to be sure about things, I can't help that.' She knelt beside his chair. 'I want you now.'

'Now. That's terrific, that's lovely, when I'm like this. Not exactly threatening like this, am I.'

'You never were threatening. I still want you, whatever you're like. I can't help it.'

Margaret kissed his eyes; licked them, kissed his forehead and his mouth.

'Don't do that.'

'But I want to.'

'Don't.'

'Why not?'

'Don't, please don't. Don't.'

Colin cried and Margaret licked at his eyes. She cradled his head.

'Darling. Ssssh. I can love you as much as I want to now and you can't stop me. You know that? You can't do a thing about it.'

'Don't.'

'I'm crazy, now, didn't you know? Anything could happen.'

'Please.'

'And I want to love you and make you better. I want to be with you. Baby. Look at me. You can still look at me. Just look at me and I'll do things for you. Please. Please. Just tell me what you'd like. Tell me what you'd like to see.'

242

'Margaret.'

'Tell me. What would you like? Would you like this? Would you?'

'You don't have to do this.'

'I'm doing it because I want to. If I stand here, near your face. Is that nice? That's for you.'

'It's nice. It is nice. But I'm – you're making me cry.'

'That's not a problem. That's fine. Put your tongue out. Please. Further. Now then, let's see.'

When Graham and Elaine came to the door, Margaret was feeding Colin on boiled egg and bread. She watched the colour leave his face as she wiped his lips.

'Who's that, are you expecting someone?'

'No.' She touched his arm and kissed him. 'I'll go and see.'

'You'll put the chain on.'

'Of course.'

Graham sat with Colin for the whole of the afternoon, reading him the papers or sitting and smoking while he took a nap. Elaine mainly stayed in the kitchen with Margaret, listening to the radio.

'That's your man, then?'

'Kind of. Yes, Elaine.'

'I've never really seen him before. He looks rotten.'

'You should have seen him in the hospital.'

'I bet. He was in the papers. My auld man looks like that every Sunday when he's sobering up. Nobody would ever notice if they took him away and nailed him to the floor.'

'No.'

'Sorry. You'll not like folk talking about it.'

'No, not really.'

'Graham doesn't know, but I've got a message for you.'

'Yes?'

'From Gus.'

'Oh.'

'I mean, he told me what he did and I think he's a total arsehole. He'll not tell any of the boys because they'll do him. Anyway, he says he's sorry.'

'Aye, I bet.'

'Lawrence said he could get a job.'

'I guessed.'

'He says he told Lawrence he could stick the job, he didn't want it any more.'

'That's a shame.'

'How?'

'At least someone would have got something out of this.'

'He's no having to work for Lawrence and he's no getting chibbed. That's better than something. I think he is sorry.'

'Tell him, that's good. I hope he does alright. Really.'

'I'll tell him.'

Elaine poured herself another mug of tea. Her hands moved neatly, lightly, arranging the milk and sugar, stirring without a sound.

'Maggie?'

'Aye?'

'What are you going to do?'

'I don't know. I was going to go to London, but I don't know. I never liked London.'

'Go down to Cardboard City, eh?'

'Could be.'

'Maggie?'

'Aye?'

'I hope you do alright.'

Margaret could think of nothing to say after that and so they sat in silence, drawing patterns in the sugar she'd spilled on the table-top. Graham stalked along the passage behind them so quietly that the sound of his voice in the room made Elaine give a little scream.

'Sorry, hen, I thought that you knew I was here. Do you have to be miserable to sit at this table or can anyone join you.'

'Sit down, Graham. I think there's still some tea. Thanks for coming. I didn't know if I'd see you before I went away.'

'I did say we wouldn't forget you. And, in fact, I'm here in an official capacity. Some of us got you this. These.'

Graham handed over a thin parcel and two envelopes.

'We thought you could stoke up inflation by causing a surge in consumer expenditure. The white envelope is a book token from the fishermen. You could use it for records, too. The other white envelope is a voucher you can spend in Marks & Spencer's. That's from the weans – they thought you could get some of that comfy Tory underwear that everyone goes on about. So there you go.'

'You haven't told her about the parcel.'

'Well, that's nothing at all. A book I had lying round the house. Descartes – you'll not feel like reading it, but it'll look good when the bailiffs come round. Talking of which, if you need a wee hand, I wouldn't like to think you were going short and not saying so.'

'Don't be daft.'

'Call it what you like – if we don't help each other there's nothing left. We know who did it, by the way.'

'Did it?'

'The wee man's accident.'

Margaret dipped her head. 'He knows who did it. He just

won't tell me. Or anyone. If you know who they are, leave them alone.'

'That's what he said.'

'It's not that he's scared. He just wants it finished. No more people getting hurt. And I agree with him. We'd rather be happy than right, you know?'

'Aye, well, we'll see. He's asleep again, through there, so you can say our goodbyes when he wakes up. We should be on our way.'

Margaret stood up to hug them both, before they left, knowing that the house would seem lonely without them, knowing that she would like them to come back.

'Listen, I'm sure Colin would like to see you again – me too. We don't get many visitors. It gets a bit tense.'

Elaine smiled and offered another motherly kiss.

'Don't worry, we'll see you soon.'

'Bye for now, hen. And remember, any help you need.'

'Still the magician.'

'Aye, something like that.'

They settled themselves as usual that night. Margaret helped Colin into her bed, saw that he had everything he might need, then went through to her sofa and the sleeping bag.

By half-past one, Margaret knew that she wouldn't sleep. She was lying on the floor, hugging one of the sofa cushions up tight to her chest. Lights looped and hopped round the walls as cars passed in the street, but mainly all the windows let in was a general, yellow haze – what the city did to moonlight.

Margaret zipped herself out of the bag and walked to the door and then opened it and stepped through. Colin's door was open, the room quite dark and still around his breathing. He murmured as she moved into the bed and inched the covers back in place. She very gently touched his back and this seemed to quiet him.

Colin woke her maybe three hours later. He was holding her more tightly than he should be able to without having pain. She could feel him looking at her in the dark.

'I knew you would be here. I knew you would be here.'

'Of course I'm here, it's alright. Be careful of your hands.'

'I need you.'

'I'm here.'

He pinned her arm against the mattress with his elbow, held her in a way that hurt.

'You don't understand. I hear music now. I go to sleep and then I hear music. I need you to be there when that happens.'

'I will be.'

'But it has to be forever. You have to stay with me forever. I can't let you go. Be with me. I think I would kill you if you went away. I think I would. Please.'

'It's alright. I'm here. Let me hold you. I'll hold you. Mind your hands.'

'They're hurting me.'

'I know. Let go.'

'Don't go away.'

'There are pills just by the bed here.'

'No! Not yet. Promise me something. Promise me.'

'What?'

'Promise first. Promise.'

'Alright, baby, alright.'

'When I'm better and I can be in my own flat you have to go away.'

'What?'

'You have to go away to London and if you're ever going to leave me, you have to do it then. Just stay away. If you come back, it has to be forever. Please. Promise.'

'I, I promise. I'll go to London. But I'll come back.'

'Go, you have to go. As soon as you can.'

'When you're well enough. Baby, you should be asleep. Let me get you a pill.'

'No, no, I'll sleep now. Stay there. Stay there and I won't hear the music. Stay there.'

Margaret lay with the damp, soft weight of his head across her shoulder. She lay, holding still, thinking she wouldn't sleep like this, that her arm was turning numb.

She knew she had been mistaken when she woke again and the morning was outside, waiting to fall through the curtains, full of birds.

Margaret has put her coat on and her case is ready. She is standing out by the door with the window pulled down, feeling the dangerous rush of air and watching the tiny slowing of the walls and junctions as they pass. Without noticing, she rubs the warm metal of her only ring and winds it around and around her finger. Her track is beginning to bind itself under others. Margaret can feel things around her mooring, rippling up to the platform's head and then growing still.

Margaret's friend Helen stands near the shops in Euston station, surrounded by arrival and departure, refusing the young men who come up and ask her for money, any spare change. She eases her weight from one hip to the other as the tannoy announces that Margaret's train is now twenty minutes late.

When Margaret does finally walk away from her train and along the platform, rather stiffly at first, she will see Helen almost at once and wave up to her. She will laugh.

Having embraced, Margaret's case uncomfortably in the way, the two women will separate. Margaret smiles and presses Helen's hand, leaves her and goes to a telephone. She calls Colin.

'Hi.'

'Hiya, how are you?'

'OK.'

'I'm later than I thought because of the train.'

'I thought that.'

'It was a good journey, though. Met some people.'

'Men?'

'One of them was, yes. I was thinking . . .'

'What?'

'I did some thinking on the way down. You know, it gives you a chance to do that. Nothing else around.'

'And what happened?'

'I'll tell you later – I'll have to go in a minute, this is all my money nearly gone. Listen, I'll be back soon. Probably Friday, I think. Can you hear me?'

'Yes. Yes, I can hear you. It would be nice if you came back. I would like that a lot.'

'Well, it'll be Friday. I would like that. Listen, I have to go, you take care.'

Margaret's money runs out before she can say goodbye.

The late sun outside the station is very strong and from a distance its doorways seem white, more like curtains of white than ways made through walls and into light. Margaret walks to one door and sinks into brilliant air, becoming first a moving shadow, then a curve, a dancing line.